Penelope  W9-ADH-318

Preface by Hermione Lee, Advisory Editor

When Penelope Fitzgerald unexpectedly won the Booker Prize with *Offshore*, in 1979, at the age of sixty-three, she said to her friends: 'I knew I was an outsider.' The people she wrote about in her novels and biographies were outsiders, too: misfits, romantic artists, hopeful failures, misunderstood lovers, orphans and oddities. She was drawn to unsettled characters who lived on the edges. She wrote about the vulnerable and the unprivileged, children, women trying to cope on their own, gentle, muddled, unsuccessful men. Her view of the world was that it divided into 'exterminators' and 'exterminatees'. She would say: 'I am drawn to people who seem to have been born defeated or even profoundly lost.' She was a humorous writer with a tragic sense of life.

Outsiders in literature were close to her heart, too. She was fond of underrated, idiosyncratic writers with distinctive voices, like the novelist J. L. Carr, or Harold Monro of the Poetry Bookshop, or the remarkable and tragic poet Charlotte Mew. The publisher Virago's enterprise of bringing neglected women writers back to life appealed to her, and under their imprint she championed the nineteenth-century novelist Margaret Oliphant. She enjoyed eccentrics like Stevie Smith. She liked writers, and people, who stood at an odd angle to the world. The child of an unusual, literary, middle-class English family, she inherited the Evangelical principles of her bishop grandfathers and the qualities of her Knox father and uncles: integrity, austerity, understatement, brilliance and a laconic, wry sense of humour.

She did not expect success, though she knew her own worth. Her writing career was not a usual one. She began publishing late in her life, around sixty, and in twenty years she published nine novels, three biographies and many essays and reviews. She changed publisher four times when she started publishing, before settling with Collins, and she never had an agent to look after her interests, though her publishers mostly became her friends and advocates. She was a dark horse, whose Booker Prize, with her third novel, was a surprise to everyone. But, by the end of her life, she had been short listed for it several times, had won a number of other British prizes, was a well-known figure on the literary scene, and became famous, at eighty, with the publication of *The Blue Flower* and its winning, in the United States, the National Book Critics Circle Award.

Yet she always had a quiet reputation. She was a novelist with a passionate following of careful readers, not a big name. She wrote compact, subtle novels. They are funny, but they are also dark. They are eloquent and clear, but also elusive and indirect. They leave a great deal unsaid. Whether she was drawing on the experiences of her own life — working for the BBC in the Blitz, helping to make a go of a small-town Suffolk bookshop, living on a leaky barge on the Thames in the 1960s, teaching children at a stage-school — or, in her last four great novels, going back in time and sometimes out of England to historical periods which she evoked with astonishing authenticity — she created whole worlds with striking economy. Her books inhabit a small space, but seem, magically, to reach out beyond it.

After her death at eighty-three, in 2000, there might have been a danger of this extraordinary voice fading away into silence and neglect. But she has been kept from oblivion by her executors and her admirers. The posthumous publication of her stories, essays and letters is now being followed by a biography (*Penelope Fitzgerald: A Life*, by Hermione Lee, Chatto & Windus, 2013), and by these very welcome reissues of her work. The fine writers who have provided introductions to these new editions show what a distinguished following she has. I hope that many new readers will now discover, and fall in love with, the work of one of the most spellbinding English novelists of the twentieth century.

From the reviews of *The Blue Flower*:

'A minor miracle of sympathy and crispness'
Adam Mars-Jones, *Guardian*

'An extraordinary imagining . . . an original masterpiece'
Hermione Lee, *Financial Times*

'*The Blue Flower* is an utterly gripping and involving novel which lingers long in the mind. I know of no contemporary writer who more exactly fulfils the brief which Lord Grey of Fallodon drafted apropos of Jane Austen ("With all these limitations you are to write, not only one novel, but several, which . . . shall be classed among the first rank of the novels written in your language in your country").

'So how *does* she do it? Is it the style? To an extent, yes, but not in any obvious way. The prose is rapid, plain and unassuming, with a fondness for dry wit and familiar allocutions. There is little imagery and no recondite vocabulary. Obliquity, timing, and the virtues of omission and allusion are her secrets. Paragraphing bears no obvious relation to temporal or spatial co-ordinates. We flit from one point of time, one view and place, with the nonchalance of a ministering yet invisible spirit.

'These are, in a sense, negative virtues, and this may be the key to the mystery. How many historical novelists seem to view the past like someone scanning a brochure of Tuscan villas in a grey November, as a foreign country where they do things not just differently but more interestingly? And when real historical figures with a known fate and stature are involved, how hard not to fall into the fallacy of assuming that they and their contemporaries were either aware of or wholly unconcerned about the figures they would cut for us, backlit by the retrospective glow which posterity has bestowed on them. Penelope Fitzgerald does not just step safely through this minefield, she makes of it a dance arena in which not only the central characters but all their numerous siblings, relatives and friends come to tumultuous and convincing life. Her past is as present, this being as "unbearably light", its search for meaning as urgent and provisional, as our own.'

Michael Dibdin, *Independent on Sunday*

'There are twenty perfectly competent novelists at work in Britain today, but only a handful producing what one could plausibly call works of literature. Of this handful, Penelope Fitzgerald possesses what one can only call the purest imagination. Her limpid, exact prose reflects an unwaveringly clear view of the human predicament. She seems to be one of those rare artists gifted with both the knowledge of how things are, and the skill to record what she knows with subtlety and devastating truthfulness.'

A. N. Wilson, *Evening Standard*

'The tension between Fitzgerald's cool and the alien turbulence of most of her characters adds piquancy . . . each one, however briefly he or she appears, is as visible and audible as the twigs scraping the windows. Fitzgerald tells you what they eat (goose, eel, cabbage, plums), what they read (if they read), and what they think about the French Revolution. It is fastidious, funny, sad, clever and very engaging.'

Gabriele Annan, *TLS*

'She is an intelligent writer, superbly and unfailingly so. But her dry wit is also allied to a great talent for emotional sympathy. The disappointment of Karoline Just ... is as terrible and as penetratingly understood as the humiliation of Chekhov's Varya rummaging for galoshes while the cherry orchard changes hands. A wise and funny novel.'

Lucy Hughes-Hallett, *Sunday Times*

'The life of Fritz von Hardenberg, the German romantic poet Novalis, might not seem a likely subject for Fitzgerald's ironic gift. In fact, the cool examination of the poet's grotesque family, all the minute historical details which are never laboured and always convincing, and the unsentimental, moving account of Fritz's slightly absurd passions are all very beautifully done. Fitzgerald never seems to try too hard; she never bullies the reader, but her dry, small-scale prose manages to produce large-scale emotional effects.'

Philip Hensher, *Mail on Sunday*

'*The Blue Flower* is a model of what historical fiction can be at its best – when the radical otherness of other times is not merely acknowledged but made integral to the fictional experience. It's also Fitzgerald at her best – elegant, inventive, hilarious, unsparing. I adore this book.'

Jonathan Franzen

By the same author

FICTION

The Golden Child

The Bookshop

Offshore

Human Voices

At Freddie's

Innocence

The Beginning of Spring

The Gate of Angels

The Means of Escape

NON-FICTION

Edward Burne-Jones

The Knox Brothers

Charlotte Mew and her Friends

A House of Air: Selected Writings

So I Have Thought of You: The Letters of Penelope Fitzgerald

The Blue Flower

Penelope Fitzgerald

FOURTH ESTATE • *London*

Fourth Estate
An imprint of HarperCollins*Publishers*
1 London Bridge Street,
London SE1 9GF

www.4thestate.co.uk

This Fourth Estate paperback edition published 2013

19

Previously published in paperback by Flamingo in 2002 and 1996
First published in Great Britain by Flamingo in 1995

Copyright © Penelope Fitzgerald 1995

Introduction © Candia McWilliam 2013

Preface © Hermione Lee 2013

Series advisory editor: Hermione Lee

Penelope Fitzgerald asserts the moral right to be
identified as the author of this work

The photographs on page 283 of Novalis's engagement ring are reproduced
by kind permission of the Museum Weissenfels/Saale

A catalogue record for this book is available from the British Library

ISBN 978-0-00-655019-8

Printed and bound by CPI Group (UK) Ltd, Croydon, CR0 4YY

MIX
Paper from
responsible sources
FSC® C007454

FSC™ is a non-profit international organisation established to promote
the responsible management of the world's forests. Products carrying the
FSC label are independently certified to assure consumers that they come
from forests that are managed to meet the social, economic and
ecological needs of present and future generations,
and other controlled sources.

Find out more about HarperCollins and the environment at
www.harpercollins.co.uk/green

Introduction

Penelope Fitzgerald, in an all-too-short autobiographical piece entitled 'Curriculum Vitae', writes that she could 'honestly say that I never shell peas in summer without thinking of Ruskin and of my grandfather'. That grandfather, like the one on her father's side, was a bishop who 'had started out with next to nothing'. He fell under the influence of Ruskin, who would describe, 'with keenest relish', the joy of shelling peas — 'the pop which assures one of a successful start, the fresh colour and scent of the juicy row within, and the pleasure of skilfully scooping the bouncing peas with one's thumb into the vessel by one's side'.

That description embodies the physical processes, the mental sequence and, always present with Penelope Fitzgerald, the effect upon the spirit that come with the playing of a phrase in music, the resolution of a mathematical problem or the manufacture of a satisfactory sentence. It has, too, a strict regard for several forms of veracity: practical, felt, aesthetic, metaphorical.

Of herself, Penelope Fitzgerald writes in the same essay, 'Well, those were my ancestors and I should like to have lived up to them. I should like to have been musical, I should like to be mathematical, and above all I should like never to have told a lie.' It's interesting that the verb form changes with the desire to be mathematical, as though there were more hope of that, as though she dismisses outright the other two, acknowledging truthfully the impossibility of true truthfulness. As for living up to them . . .

The Blue Flower (1995), her last novel, burdened often, and very often by other novelists, including this one, with words as inexact and lumpy as 'masterpiece' and 'genius', addresses the short shining transit of the life of the philosopher and poet Friedrich von Hardenberg (1772–1801), later to take the name Novalis, author of *Hymns to the Night* and of a novel, *Heinrich von Ofterdingen*, that contains mention of 'the blue flower', an idea of profound importance to the philosopher-poets of that mind-crowded time and place. He was author of much more, work that strives (to put it over-simply) to reconcile observable phenomena with a sublime principle.

'Mathematics is human reason itself in a form everyone can recognise. Why should poetry, reason and religion not be higher forms of Mathematics? All that is needed is a grammar of their common language.' These thoughts are put in the mind of Hardenberg by Fitzgerald, who discovers in this book something approaching that common language, in its poetry, its reason and its spirit.

The eldest of a large family, Hardenberg appeared at the start to be dull but turned out to be quite brilliant. His life was full of such flips of transfiguration, dark to light to dark again. This making light out of the dark is repeatedly effected by Fitzgerald, who has turned into this novel his, definingly Romantic, life. She has kept throughout a certain Germanness of diction, acutely listened out for rather than inserted: articles sit in front of some proper nouns; no word or phrase is offered in the German without setting a crumb-trail worth following.

Penelope Fitzgerald is a novelist who elevates her readers through teaching them how to read her. She freely offers her own great intelligence to all her readers, as to her humblest protagonist. Her approach to her material is interior, never merely the stretching of an aestheticised membrane over prefigured event. To see her manuscript is to confirm what the finished artefact has told us: in her rounded yet italic hand, each letter sits in its row like a bead on the abacus of straight thought, doing the exact work its position and character demands. The miracle is that these beads are also as alive as peas, to be sown and set, fertile, tender, reaching, tenacious, and when harvested and dried down as hard as hail throwing itself at the window in the reader's head. She does not strew effect, uses shock sparingly and administers it – often violently – through silence, a woven veil or a sideways unrequited look.

Hardenberg's position in the minor Saxon nobility of the late eighteenth century had limited opportunities. His family had estates, a household, a respectable allocation of linen, duties, a nag or two, habits of generosity; not money. The father was a devout adherent of the Moravian Church, a Christocentric group of a certain spiritual climate, dwelling (in the words of Penelope Fitzgerald's uncle Ronald Knox) with monotonous sentimentalism, 'only less distressing in German than in English', on the wound in Christ's side.

Other modes of thought, though, are stirring, and not far off. At Jena, one of the universities attended by Hardenberg, Goethe walks along in plain view, an old man of over forty. Schelling, Hegel and Hölderlin lodge together. The philosopher Fichte and the Romantic Schlegel teach Hardenberg. *Fichtieren*, to romanticise Fichte-style, is a fashion among the students. At one point, there is a duelling accident. Two good-sized bits of finger are lopped off. Fritz's medical student friend Dietmahler makes him carry the part-fingers for safekeeping in the ideal receptacle that is his mouth. One has a heavy ring. Can you unfeel that? The novelist has transmitted to the reader the very taste of subjectivity.

Hardenberg was sent to learn from Kreisamtmann Coelestin Just the business of overseeing the processes of the mining of salt, in order to make a living beyond that of the savourless life of a writer-scholar. By this point he already has the inter-mittent transformative sense that beauty is where it falls; that everything is illuminated.

Trying to assemble information for her projected life of L. P. Hartley, Penelope Fitzgerald interviewed Princess Clary, who said, 'My dear, how can you write the life of a writer? If he had entered into politics, if he had commanded an army in warfare, but what life can a writer have?'

A chance visit, paid in the company of Just, to a family as large as his own but more prone to laughter, changed Fritz von Hardenberg's life.

He fell in love with Sophie von Kuhn when she was twelve. We first see her, an ordinary enough girl, standing at a window wishing for something to happen, be it only a fall of snow.

We are given Sophie in full: she is impious, ordinary-looking, greedy, fond of fart and sex jokes. She has nice hair and dark eyes – like those of Raphael in the self-portrait he made at twenty-five. We never doubt her lover's transforming serious love of and for her. We too come to see and to care, in the irrational incremental way of love. This short book induces in its reader many forms of the topple into love: with big families, with children, with 'the one', 'the other', with an idea, with thought, with nature.

The blue flower, signifying that elusive thing which can connect the individual self to an understanding of greater external existence, finds its equivalent in the novel which itself is a concrete rendering of the abstraction it contemplates. *The Blue Flower* constitutes for its reader a blue flower. Hardenberg came to call Sophie his Philosophy. This, to a novelist of such metaphysical mind, must have been a folding together of concept and embodiment impossible to resist.

'As a hopelessly addicted writer of short books I have to

try to see to it that every confrontation and every dialogue has some reference to what I hope will be understood as the heart of the novel,' Penelope Fitzgerald writes, three years before her death. She is pinning the numberless stars in their places with each word written, and calling them each by their names. She is very clear here about why, but how does she see so feelingly – and set it down?

Penelope Fitzgerald was in the provident habit of unravelling and reknitting garments for her family ('I have unpicked the famous red gloves and am knitting them up again for you!' she writes to her daughter Maria in 1972). That curative use of 'up' is surely Shakespearean. And this 'knitting up' is what she does with her areas of preoccupation (it's too simple to call it research) and her novels.

She embodies and suggests, giving a life to the physical such that it radiates metaphysically. Stars, in all their forms, are here, from dust (Novalis's first book was *Blutenstaub*, that is *Pollen*, a rich dust) to light, through the stellar forms of snowflakes and the squarer salt crystals arriving under sunlight in low pans with the stealth of frost-flowers, the 'sparkling chatter of the harpsichord'. Here is, also, the violent entropic subtraction of death in youth, leaving a burnt place behind in the creation – a bright star gone – the graphic bursting bark of a human cough never far away as the white death of consumption awaits within. Sentences capturing, describing, transmuting, extinguishing or measuring light (with cypress shadows) are equalled in number by those that describe darkness or concealment, either social or, dreadfully, anatomical, the dark of the body where tumours assemble themselves and the blood waits to declare itself on linen. This light into darkness, dark into light is a faithful mirroring by the novelist.

It is not fantastical or worked up, not 'heightened' at all, although a German for 'imagination' is *Fantasie*. In dealing with such matters it is hard to avoid a kind of tense, high, exalted note used by prose-technicians who may wish to ramp up mood or emotion. But in this novel, the increments by which we are led in these new lives through their autumn and 'forewinter' and tipped into a deep grief show a novelist and a character devoid of kitsch. She plucks life of its feathery detail, as with the geese at Tennstedt, stripped of their down alive twice before slaughter.

As Penelope Fitzgerald writes in *Charlotte Mew and her Friends*, 'Terminal illness is a great simplifier of daily life, everything being reduced to the same point of hope against hope.' That sense of intensified life we swear after disaster that we will cleave to, Fitzgerald manages to keep alive yet sweetly unhectic in her writing.

The very structure of the book is constellated. Each short chapter of the fifty-five works with what has been and what will be so that we see the unavoidability of what supervenes for each character, as we see stars where once they were; stars might be said to be, as we observe them, fictions. Because we understand more than we know ourselves to, on account of the work the author has done to hold us in perfect trust, we feel an accretive ache as each character moves towards her or his fate; suddenly we have 'known all along'. When we reread, the urge to hold it back, as in life, beats stark. We are given to 'know' subconsciously what we cannot know with our whole mind because the novelist has fully imagined each person who arrives; each carries his fate, as we each do, within our own allotted time.

That these are people who have lived, who are not 'made up', is of less rather than more help to a novelist unless she be one of deep imagination and assimilated learning. Bones ground to make novelistic bread often stick in the reader's craw. It is one of the objections dearly held by those who hold 'historical novels' in contempt. Some fun is had in this novel at the expense of those unimaginative self-designated realists who think that artists are tricksy prestidigitators.

Certain conditions prevail in *The Blue Flower.* Time is short. You may be betrothed at twice seven, worn out by nursing and marriage at three times seven, off the market at twenty-eight. Men, too, have a tight span in which to be and to act. New babies are born annually to married women; some, in the way of it, die. Pregnant women who are unmarried may visit the 'Angel-Maker' to resolve things. Angels offer annoyance or solace in fraternal or in spirit form. Fritz sees one such spirit and sometimes wishes he saw rather less of another angel more robust and accident-prone; he will get his undesired wish. As he has occasion later to say, 'If a story begins with finding, it must end with searching.'

Children speak no pappy or truncated language here but utter their thoughts; there is no time for the approximations of baby talk in a world where revolution is massing in France, and Buonaparte is making himself felt. For Fritz's six-year-old brother, 'the Bernhard', thought is blood, as Fitzgerald has it in *The Gate of Angels.*

The great are teased. In a world where linen is counted, Goethe has two overcoats on account of his fear of draughts and no small talk to spare even for the mortally sick Sophie von Kuhn, who is reduced to 'venturing that Jena is a larger town than Grüningen'. Goethe is sententious and a bit creepy about Sophie to Fritz's brother Erasmus. The great poet has forgotten perhaps the transformative nature of love, that can make of a potato-fed (or bread-and-butter-fed) girl of human clay a persisting star in the mind of a man. He cannot 'read' that it is not for Fritz, his brother, that Erasmus cares, but for Fritz's intended, for he too has fallen in love with Sophie. There is love surplus and love unmet to twist the heart in this novel. The lonely consequence of sparing your loved one's feelings are terribly demonstrated by Karoline Just, who gives life to a man who has never existed, to spare Hardenberg pain for not loving her as she loves him.

But they are Saxons, these characters, and know how to make a good dinner even if their hearts are breaking. Itemised meals that seem to mean something else, like auguries, arrive in their season: cherries dark as leaves or starlings, the amarelles for Kirsch the darkest of all, fiery schnaps flavoured with peppermint, all the better for the seething of a pig's neck fat, ears and nostrils.

'Let time stand still until she turns around,' thinks Fritz, first beholding his love, in tune with his heartbeat. In so seasonal, worshipful and abbreviated a way of life, music is never far away; we hear even the piano's (possibly not yet invented) third pedal at Fritz and Sophie's engagement party.

So suggestive with extraneous spirits is this chapter, in which a sudden and opinionated first person arrives just the once, to remark upon an unidentifiable snatch of music amid the Bach and hymns by Zinzendorf, that it is as though we are for one moment let into a secret within the secret; we hear and see ghosts. But we cannot know what it is. We know merely that, should we develop further capacity to imagine, we would see – albeit briefly – 'something', quite clearly. We are looking for the blue flower.

By now we may have suspicions as to its nature; even if we are right, what is to say that death cannot be changed, by being thought about otherwise, by the turn from dark into light; is not the dark its own kind of light?

There is little sense that this other way of thinking must necessarily involve Christ. The clergy come in for less of the satire for which their visits to the house of fiction have primed them; idle, vain and unfeeling doctors receive the brunt with their casual cruelty and patronising cant, and a landlady whose dithery taste for the pain of others is gratified in a harsh moment of authorial grip and withdrawal of anything but Sophie's pain imagined by the inextricably involved reader. We are thrown onto our expertly readied imaginations and we flinch, writhe, do not credit, accept; and have to go on.

No character is trapped in the place the novelist has made for him. They walk, and the floorboards creak, they breathe and the window mists, they live and love and die, in Sophie's case with her repeatedly reopened wound kept open still, to release the backed-up poison, with the use of a worked silk thread. Sheets, wearing thin, turned sides to middle, by now a colour milder than white, through which the broad summer sunshine may be seen, outlive the human souls whom we met first amid a great laundering.

Just as there is no self-regarding plangency of tone, there is no officious marshalling of characters. No points are laboured; all are sharp, and let the light in. Sophie's first agony arrives in the form of something that glitters. The novelist with her surgical haberdashery is keeping our reading wound fresh. She offers no anaesthetic but clarity and beauty.

Returning from what will be his last visit to his mortally sick Philosophy, Hardenberg approaches his family home. He is late. 'Fritz paid the fine which was collected from all latecomers.'

It is the fine that we are here to pay again and again, the price of love.

Penelope Fitzgerald lives up to her ancestors.

Candia McWilliam
2013

Contents

1 WASHDAY 1

2 THE STUDY 7

3 THE BERNHARD 11

4 BERNHARD'S RED CAP 15

5 THE HISTORY OF FREIHERR HEINRICH
VON HARDENBERG 21

6 UNCLE WILHELM 26

7 THE FREIHERR AND THE FRENCH REVOLUTION 31

8 IN JENA 37

9 AN INCIDENT IN STUDENT LIFE 43

10 A QUESTION OF MONEY 47

11 A DISAGREEMENT 50

12 THE SENSE OF IMMORTALITY 55

13 THE JUST FAMILY 60

14 FRITZ AT TENNSTEDT 65

15	JUSTEN	69
16	THE JENA CIRCLE	73
17	WHAT IS THE MEANING?	75
18	THE ROCKENTHIENS	80
19	A QUARTER OF AN HOUR	86
20	THE NATURE OF DESIRE	91
21	SNOW	95
22	NOW LET ME GET TO KNOW HER	99
23	I CAN'T COMPREHEND HER	108
24	THE BROTHERS	112
25	CHRISTMAS AT WEISSENFELS	116
26	THE MANDELSLOH	123
27	ERASMUS CALLS ON KAROLINE JUST	129
28	FROM SOPHIE'S DIARY, 1795	133
29	A SECOND READING	135
30	SOPHIE'S LIKENESS	142
31	I COULD NOT PAINT HER	147
32	THE WAY LEADS INWARDS	155
33	AT JENA	160
34	THE GARDEN-HOUSE	164
35	SOPHIE IS COLD THROUGH AND THROUGH	168
36	DR HOFRAT EBHARD	171

37	WHAT IS PAIN?	174
38	KAROLINE AT GRÜNINGEN	177
39	THE QUARREL	182
40	HOW TO RUN A SALT MINE	185
41	SOPHIE AT FOURTEEN	192
42	THE FREIFRAU IN THE GARDEN	198
43	THE ENGAGEMENT PARTY	207
44	THE INTENDED	216
45	SHE MUST GO TO JENA	226
46	VISITORS	229
47	HOW PROFESSOR STARK MANAGED	238
48	TO SCHLÖBEN	245
49	AT THE ROSE	251
50	A DREAM	258
51	AUTUMN 1796	262
52	ERASMUS IS OF SERVICE	265
53	A VISIT TO MAGISTER KEGEL	268
54	ALGEBRA, LIKE LAUDANUM, DEADENS PAIN	271
55	MAGISTER KEGEL'S LESSON	274
	AFTERWORD	281

Author's Note

This novel is based on the life of Friedrich von Hardenberg (1772–1801) before he became famous under the name Novalis. All his surviving work, letters from and to him, the diaries and official and private documents, were published by W. Kohlhammer Verlag in five volumes between 1960 and 1988. The original editors were Richard Samuel and Paul Kluckhohn, and I should like to acknowledge the debt I owe to them.

The description of an operation without an anaesthetic is mostly taken from Fanny d'Arblay's letter to her sister Esther Burney (September 30, 1811) about her mastectomy.

'Novels arise out of the shortcomings of history.'

F. von Hardenberg, later Novalis,
Fragmente und Studien, 1799–1800

1

Washday

JACOB Dietmahler was not such a fool that he could not see that they had arrived at his friend's home on the washday. They should not have arrived anywhere, certainly not at this great house, the largest but two in Weissenfels, at such a time. Dietmahler's own mother supervised the washing three times a year, therefore the household had linen and white underwear for four months only. He himself possessed eighty-nine shirts, no more. But here, at the Hardenberg house in Kloster Gasse, he could tell from the great dingy snowfalls of sheets, pillow-cases, bolster-cases, vests, bodices, drawers, from the upper windows into the courtyard, where grave-looking servants, both men and women, were receiving them into giant baskets, that they washed only once a year. This might not mean wealth, in fact he knew that in this case it didn't, but it was certainly an indication of long standing. A numerous family, also. The under-wear of children and young persons, as well as the larger sizes, fluttered through the blue air, as though the children themselves had taken to flight.

'Fritz, I'm afraid you have brought me here at an inconvenient moment. You should have let me know. Here I am, a stranger to your honoured family, knee deep in your smallclothes.'

'How can I tell when they're going to wash?' said Fritz. 'Anyway, you're a thousand times welcome at all times.'

'The Freiherr is trampling on the unsorted garments,' said the housekeeper, leaning out of one of the first-floor windows.

'Fritz, how many are there in your family?' asked Dietmahler. 'So many things?' Then he shouted suddenly: 'There is no such concept as a thing in itself!'

Fritz, leading the way across the courtyard, stopped, looked round and then in a voice of authority shouted back: 'Gentlemen! Look at the washbasket! Let your thought be the washbasket! Have you thought the washbasket? Now then, gentlemen, let your thought be on *that* that thought the washbasket!'

Inside the house the dogs began to bark. Fritz called out to one of the basket-holding servants: 'Are my father and mother at home?' But it was not worth it, the mother was always at home. There came out into the courtyard a short, unfinished looking young man, even younger than Fritz, and a fair-haired girl. 'Here, at any rate, are my brother Erasmus and my sister Sidonie. Nothing else is wanted while they are here.'

Both threw themselves on Fritz. 'How many are there of you altogether?' asked Dietmahler again. Sidonie gave him her hand, and smiled.

'Here among the table-linen, I am disturbed by Fritz Hardenberg's young sister,' thought Dietmahler. 'This is the sort of thing I meant to avoid.'

She said, 'Karl will be somewhere, and Anton, and the Bernhard, but of course there are more of us.' In the house, seeming of less substance even than the shadows, was Freifrau von Hardenberg. 'Mother,' said Fritz, 'this is Jacob Dietmahler, who studied in Jena at the same time as myself and Erasmus, and now he is a Deputy Assistant to the Professor of Medicine.'

'Not quite yet,' said Dietmahler. 'I hope, one day.'

'You know I have been in Jena to look up my friends,' went on Fritz. 'Well, I have asked him to stay a few days with us.' The Freifrau looked at him with what seemed to be a gleam of terror, a hare's wild look. 'Dietmahler needs a little brandy, just to keep him alive for a few hours.'

'He is not well?' asked the Freifrau in dismay. 'I will send for the housekeeper.' 'But we don't need her,' said Erasmus. 'You have your own keys to the dining room surely.' 'Surely I have,' she said, looking at him imploringly. 'No, I have them,' said Sidonie. 'I have had them ever since my sister was married. I will take you all to the pantry, think no more about it.' The Freifrau, recollecting herself, welcomed her son's friend to the house. 'My husband cannot receive you just at this moment, he is at prayer.' Relieved that the ordeal was over, she did not accompany them through the shabby rooms and even shabbier corridors, full of plain old workmanlike furniture. On the plum-coloured walls were discoloured rectangles where pictures must once have hung. In the pantry Sidonie poured the cognac and Erasmus proposed the toast to Jena. '*Stosst an! Jena lebe hoch! Hurra!*'

'What the Hurra is for I don't know,' said Sidonie. 'Jena is a place where Fritz and Asmus wasted money, caught lice, and listened to nonsense from philosophers.' She gave the pantry keys to her brothers and went back to her mother, who was standing at the precise spot where she had been left, staring out at the preparations for the great wash. 'Mother, I want you to entrust me with a little money, let us say five or six thaler, so that I can make some further arrangements for our guest.' 'My dear, what arrangements? There is already a bed in the room he is to have.' 'Yes, but the servants store the candles there, and they read the Bible there during their free hour.' 'But my dear, why should this man want to go to his room during the day?' Sidonie thought that he might want to do some writing. 'Some writing!' repeated her mother, in utter bewilderment. 'Yes, and for that he should have a table.' Sidonie pressed home her advantage. 'And, in case he should like to wash, a jug of water and a basin, yes, and a slop-pail.' 'But Sidonie, will he not know how to wash under the pump? Your brothers all wash so.' 'And there is no chair in the room, where he might put his clothes at night.' 'His clothes! It is still far too cold to undress at night. I have not undressed myself at night, even in summer, for I think twelve years.' 'And yet you've given birth to eight of us!' cried Sidonie. 'God in heaven spare me a marriage like yours!'

The Freifrau scarcely heeded her. 'And there is another thing, you have not thought – the Father may raise his voice.' This did not perturb Sidonie. 'This Dietmahler must get used to the Father, and to the way we do things, otherwise let him pack up and go straight home.'

'But in that case, cannot he get used to our guest-rooms? Fritz should have told him that we lead a plain, God-fearing life.'

'Why is it God-fearing not to have a slop-pail?' asked Sidonie.

'What are these words? Are you ashamed of your home, Sidonie?'

'Yes, I am.' She was fifteen, burning like a flame. Impatience, translated into spiritual energy, raced through all the young Hardenbergs. Fritz now wished to take his friend down to the river to walk up the towpath and talk of poetry and the vocation of man. 'This we could have done anywhere,' said Dietmahler. 'But I want you to see my home,' Fritz told him. 'It is old-fashioned, we are old-fashioned in Weissenfels, but we have peace, it is *heimisch*.' One of the servants who had been in the courtyard, dressed now in a dark cloth coat, appeared in the doorway and said that the Master would be glad to see his son's guest in the study, before dinner.

'The old enemy is in his lair,' shouted Erasmus.

Dietmahler felt a certain awkwardness. 'I shall be honoured to meet your father,' he told Fritz.

2

The Study

IT was Erasmus who must take after his father, for the Freiherr, politely rising to his feet in the semi-darkness of his study, was unexpectedly a small stout man wearing a flannel nightcap against the draughts. Where then did Fritz — since his mother was no more than a shred — get his awkward leanness from, and his height? But the Freiherr had this in common with his eldest son, that he started talking immediately, his thoughts seizing the opportunity to become words.

'Gracious sir, I have come to your house,' Dietmahler began nervously, but the Freiherr interrupted, 'This is not my house. It is true I bought it from the widow of von Pilsach to accommodate my family when I was appointed Director of the Salt Mining Administration of Saxony, which necessitated my living in Weissenfels. But the Hardenberg property, our true home and lands, are in Oberwiederstadt, in the county of Mansfeld.' Dietmahler said politely that he wished he had been fortunate enough to go to Oberwiederstadt. 'You would have seen nothing but ruins,' said the Freiherr, 'and insufficiently fed cattle. But they are ancestral lands, and it is for this reason that it is important to know, and I am now taking the opportunity of asking you, whether it is true that my eldest son, Friedrich, has entangled himself with a young woman of the middle classes.'

'I've heard nothing about his entangling himself with anyone,' said Dietmahler indignantly, 'but in any case, I doubt if he can be judged by ordinary standards, he is a poet and a philosopher.'

'He will earn his living as an Assistant Inspector of Salt Mines,' said the Freiherr, 'but I see that it is not right to interrogate you. I welcome you as a guest, therefore as another son, and you will not mind my finding out a little more about you. What is your age, and what do you intend to do in life?'

'I am two and twenty and I am training to become a surgeon.'

'And are you dutiful to your father?'

'My father is dead, Freiherr. He was a plasterer.'

'I did not ask you that. Have you known what it was to have sad losses in your family life?'

'Yes, sir, I have lost two little brothers from scarlet fever and a sister from consumption, in the course of one year.'

The Freiherr took off his nightcap, apparently out of respect. 'A word of advice. If, as a young man, a student, you are tormented by a desire for women, it is best to get out into the fresh air as much as possible.' He took a turn round the room, which was lined with book-cases, some with empty shelves. 'Meanwhile, how much would you expect to spend in a week on spirits, hey? How much on books – not books of devotion, mind you? How much on a new black coat, without any explanation as to how the old one has ceased to be wearable? How much, hey?'

'Freiherr, you are asking me these questions as a criticism of your son. Yet you have just said that you were not going to interrogate me.'

Hardenberg was not really an old man – he was between fifty and sixty – but he stared at Jacob Dietmahler with an old man's drooping neck and lowered head. 'You are right, quite right. I took the opportunity. Opportunity, after all, is only another word for temptation.'

He put his hand on his guest's shoulder. Dietmahler, alarmed, did not know whether he was being pushed down or whether the Freiherr was leaning on him, perhaps both. Certainly he must be used to entrusting his weight to someone more competent, perhaps to his strong sons, perhaps even to his daughter. Dietmahler felt his clavicle giving way. I am cutting a mean figure, he thought, but at least he was on his knees, while Hardenberg, annoyed at his own weakness, steadied himself as he sank down by grasping first at the corner of the solid oak table, then at one of its legs. The door opened and the same servant returned, but this time in carpet slippers.

'Does the Freiherr wish the stove to be made up?'

'Kneel with us, Gottfried.'

Down creaked the old man by the master. They looked like an old married couple nodding over their household accounts together, even more so when the Freiherr exclaimed, 'Where are the little ones?'

'The servants' children, Excellency?'

'Certainly, and the Bernhard.'

3

The Bernhard

In the Hardenbergs' house there was an angel, August Wilhelm Bernhard, fair as wheat. After plain motherly Charlotte, the eldest, pale, wide-eyed Fritz, stumpy little Erasmus, easy-going Karl, open-hearted Sidonie, painstaking Anton, came the blonde Bernhard. To his mother, the day when he had to be put into breeches was terrible. She who hardly ever, if at all, asked anything for herself, implored Fritz. 'Go to him, go to your Father, beg him, pray him, to let my Bernhard continue a little longer in his frocks.' 'Mother, what can I say, I think Bernhard is six years old.'

He was now more than old enough, Sidonie thought, to understand politeness to a visitor. 'I do not know how long he will stay, Bernhard. He has brought quite a large valise.'

'His valise is full of books,' said the Bernhard, 'and he has also brought a bottle of schnaps. I dare say he thought there would not be such a thing in our house.'

'Bernhard, you have been in his room.'

'Yes, I went there.'

'You have opened his valise.'

'Yes, just to see his things.'

'Did you leave it open, or did you shut it again?'

The Bernhard hesitated. He could not remember.

'Well, it doesn't signify,' said Sidonie. 'You must, of course, confess to Herr Dietmahler what you have done, and ask his pardon.'

'When?'

'It should be before nightfall. In any case, there is no time like the present.'

'I've nothing to tell him!' cried the Bernhard. 'I haven't spoiled his things.'

'You know that Father punishes you very little,' said Sidonie coaxingly. 'Not as we were punished. Perhaps he will tell you to wear your jacket the wrong way out for a few days, only to remind you. We shall have some music before supper and after that I will go with you up to the visitor and you can take his hand and speak to him quietly.'

'I'm sick of this house!' shouted the Bernhard, snatching himself away.

Fritz was in the kitchen garden patrolling the vegetable beds, inhaling the fragrance of the broad bean flowers, reciting at the top of his voice.

'Fritz,' Sidonie called to him. 'I have lost the Bernhard.'

'Oh, that can't be.'

'I was reproving him in the morning room, and he escaped from me and jumped over the window-sill and into the yard.'

'Have you sent one of the servants?'

'Oh, Fritz, best not, they will tell Mother.'

Fritz looked at her, shut his book and said he would go out and find his brother. 'I will drag him back by the hair if necessary, but you and Asmus will have to entertain my friend.'

'Where is he now?'

'He is in his room, resting. Father has worn him out. By the way, his room has been turned upside down and his valise is open.'

'Is he angry?'

'Not at all. He thinks perhaps that it's one of our customs at Weissenfels.'

Fritz put on his frieze-coat and went without hesitation down to the river. Everyone in Weissenfels knew that young Bernhard would never drown, because he was a water-rat. He couldn't swim, but then neither could his father. During his seven years' service with the Hanoverian army the Freiherr had seen action repeatedly and crossed many rivers, but had never been put to the necessity of swimming. Bernhard, however, had always lived close to water and seemed not to be able to live without it. Down by the ferry he was forever hanging about, hoping to slip on board without paying his three pfennig for the crossing. The parents did not know this. There was a kind of humane conspiracy in the town to keep many matters from the Freiherr, in order to spare his piety on the one hand, and on the other, not to provoke his ferocious temper.

The sun was down, only the upper sky glowed. The mist was walking up the water. The little boy was not at the ferry. A few pigs and a flock of geese, forbidden to go by way of Weissenfels' handsome bridge, were waiting for the last crossing.

4

Bernhard's Red Cap

FOR the first time Fritz felt afraid. His imagination ran ahead of him, back to the Kloster Gasse, meeting the housekeeper at the front door — but, young master, what is that load you are carrying into the house? It is dripping everywhere, the floors, I am responsible for them.

His mother had always believed that the Bernhard was destined to become a page, if not at the court of the Elector of Saxony, then perhaps with the Count of Mansfeld or the Duke of Braunschweig-Wolfenbüttel. One of Fritz's duties, before long, would be to drag his little brother round these various courts in the hope of placing him satisfactorily.

The rafts lay below the bridge, close into the bank, alongside piles of gently heaving, chained pinewood logs, waiting for the next stage in their journey. A watchman was trying a bunch of keys in the door of a hut. 'Herr Watchman, have you seen a boy running?'

A boy was supposed to come with his dinner, said the watchman, but he was a rascal and had not come. 'Look, the towpath is empty.'

The empty barges laid up for repair were moored at their station on the opposite bank. Fritz pelted over the bridge. Everyone saw him, coat flying. Had the Freiherr no servants to send? The barges wallowed on their mooring ropes, grating against each other, strake against strake. From the quayside Fritz jumped down about four feet or so onto the nearest deck. There was a scurrying, as though of an animal larger than a dog.

'Bernhard!'

'I will never come back,' Bernhard called.

The child ran across the deck, and then, afraid to risk the drop onto the next boat, climbed over the gunwale and then stayed there hanging on with both hands, scrabbling with his boots for a foothold. Fritz caught hold of him by the wrists and at the same moment the whole line of barges made one of their unaccountable shifts, heaving grossly towards each other, so that the Bernhard, still hanging, was trapped and squeezed. A pitiful cough and a burst of tears and blood were forced out of him like air out of a balloon.

'How am I going to get you out of here?' demanded Fritz. 'What a pest you are, what a pest.'

'Let me go, let me die!' wheezed the Bernhard.

'We'll have to work our way along forward, then I can pull you up.' But the instinct to preserve life seemed for the moment to have deserted the child, Fritz must do it all, dragging and shuffling him along, wildly protesting, between the two gunwales. If they had been on the other bank there would have been passers-by to lend a hand, but then, Fritz thought, they'd think murder was being done. The boats grew narrower, he saw the glimmering water idling beneath them and hauled the child up like a wet sack. His face was not pale, but a brilliant crimson.

'Make an effort, do you want to drown?'

'What would it matter if I did?' squeaked the Bernhard. 'You said once that death was not significant, but only a change in condition.'

'Drat you, you've no business to understand that,' Fritz shouted in his ear.

'My *Mütze!*'

The child was much attached to his red cap, which was missing. So, too were one of his front teeth and his breeches. He had on only long cotton drawers tied with tape. Like most rescuers, Fritz felt suddenly furious with the loved and saved. 'Your *Mütze* has gone, it must be on its way to the Elbe by now.' Then, ashamed of his anger, he picked the little boy up and put him on his shoulders to carry him home. The Bernhard, aloft, revived a little. 'Can I wave at the people?'

Fritz had to make his way to the end of the line of barges, where perpendicular iron steps had been built into one bank and he could climb up without putting down the Bernhard.

How heavy a child is when it gives up responsibility.

He couldn't go straight back to the Kloster Gasse like this. But Sidonie and Asmus between them would be equal to explaining things away during the before-dinner music. Meanwhile, in Weissenfels, he had many places to get dry. After crossing the bridge again he walked only a short way along the Saale and then took two turns to the left and one to the right, where the lights were now shining in Severin's bookshop.

There were no customers in the shop. The pale Severin, in his long overall, was examining one of the tattered lists, which booksellers prefer to all other reading, by the light of a candle fitted with a reflector.

'Dear Hardenberg! I did not expect you. Put the little brother, I pray you, on a sheet of newspaper. Here is yesterday's *Leipziger Zeitung*.' He was surprised at nothing.

'The little brother is in disgrace,' said Fritz, depositing the Bernhard. 'He ran down onto the barges. How he came to get quite so wet I don't know.'

'*Kinderleicht, kinderleicht*,' said Severin indulgently, but his indulgence was for Fritz. He could not warm to children, since all of them were scribblers in books. He went to the very back of the shop, opened a wooden chest, and took out a large knitted shawl, a peasant thing.

'Take off your shirt, I will wrap you in this,' he said. 'Your brother need not return it to me. Why did you cause all this trouble? Did you hope to sail away and leave your father and mother behind you?'

'Of course not,' said the Bernhard scornfully. 'All the boats on that mooring are under repair. They could not sail, they have no canvas. I did not want to sail, I wanted to drown.'

'That I don't believe,' replied Severin, 'and I should have preferred you not to say it.'

'He loves water,' said Fritz, impelled to defend his own.

'Evidently.'

'And, indeed, so do I,' Fritz cried. 'Water is the most wonderful element of all. Even to touch it is a pleasure.'

Perhaps Severin did not find it a pleasure to have quite so much water on the floor of his bookshop. He was a man of forty-five, 'old' Severin to Fritz, a person of great good sense, unperturbed by life's contingencies. He had been poor and unsuccessful, had kept himself going by working very hard, at low wages, for the proprietor of the bookshop, and then, when the proprietor had died, had married his widow and come into the whole property. Of course the whole of Weissenfels knew this and approved of it. It was their idea of wisdom exactly.

Poetry, however, meant a great deal to Severin — almost as much as his lists. He would have liked to see his young friend Hardenberg continue as a poet without the necessity of working as a salt mine inspector.

For the rest of his journey home the Bernhard continued to complain about the loss of his red *Mütze*. It was the only thing he had possessed which indicated his revolutionary sympathies.

'I don't know how you got hold of it,' Fritz told him. 'And if Father had ever caught sight of it he would in any case have told the servants to throw it on the rubbish heap. Let all this be a lesson to you to keep yourself from poking about among the visitors' possessions.'

'In a republic there would be no possessions,' said the Bernhard.

5

The History of Freiherr Heinrich
Von Hardenberg

FREIHERR von Hardenberg was born in 1738, and while
he was still a boy came into the properties of Oberwiederstadt on the River Wipper in the county of Mansfeld,
and the manor and farm of Schlöben-bei-Jena. During
the Seven Years' War he served, as a loyal subject, in the
Hanoverian Legion. After the Peace of Paris he gave up
his commission. And he married, but in 1769 there was
an epidemic of smallpox in the towns along the Wipper,
and his young wife died. The Freiherr nursed the infected
and the dying, and those whose families could not afford
a grave were buried in the grounds of Oberwiederstadt
which, having once been a convent, still had some conse-
crated earth. He had undergone a profound religious
conversion – but I have not! said Erasmus, as soon as he
was old enough to ask about the rows of green mounds
so close to the house. 'I have not – does he ever think
of that?'

On each grave was a plain headstone, carved with the
words: *He, or she, was born on——, and on——returned home*. This

was the inscription preferred by the Moravians. The Freiherr now worshipped with the Moravian Brethren, for whom every soul is either dead, awakened, or converted. A human soul is converted as soon as it realises that it is in danger, and what that danger is, and hears itself cry aloud, *He is my Lord.*

A little over a year after his wife's death the Freiherr married his young cousin Bernadine von Böltzig. 'Bernadine, what an absurd name! Have you no other?' Yes, her second name was Auguste. 'Well, I shall call you Auguste henceforward.' In his gentler moments, she was Gustel. Auguste, though timorous, proved fertile. After twelve months the first daughter, Charlotte, was born, and a year later, Fritz. 'When the time comes for their education,' the Freiherr said, 'both shall be sent to the Brethren at Neudietendorf.'

Neudietendorf, between Erfurt and Gotha, was a colony of the Herrnhut. The Herrnhut was the centre where fifty years earlier the Moravians, refugees from persecution, had been allowed to settle down in peace. To the Moravians, a child is born into an ordered world into which he must fit. Education is concerned with the status of the child in the kingdom of God.

Neudietendorf, like the Herrnhut, was a place of tranquillity. Wind instruments, instead of bells, summoned the children to their classes. It was also a place of total obedience, for the meek are the inheritors. They must always go about in threes, so that the third might tell the Prediger what the other two had found to talk about. On the other hand, no teacher might give a punishment while he was still angry, since an unjust punishment is never forgotten.

The children swept the floors, tended the animals and made the hay, but they were never allowed to strive against each other, or take part in competitive games. They received thirty hours a week of education and religious instruction. All must be in bed by sunset, and remain silent until they got up at five the next morning. After any communal task had been completed − say, whitewashing the henhouses − the long trestle tables were brought out for a 'love-feast', when all sat down together, hymns were sung and a small glass of home-made liqueur was handed to everyone, even the youngest. The boarding fees were eight thaler for a girl, ten thaler for a boy (who ate more, and needed a Latin and a Hebrew grammar).

Charlotte von Hardenberg, the eldest, who took after her mother, did very well at the House of Maidens. She married early, and had gone to live in Lausitz. Fritz had been born a dreamy, seemingly backward little boy. After a serious illness when he was nine years old, he became intelligent and in the same year was despatched to Neudietendorf. 'But in what has he fallen short?' demanded the Freiherr, when only a few months later he was requested by the Prediger, on behalf of the Elders, to take his son away. The Prediger, who was very unwilling to condemn any child absolutely, explained that Fritz perpetually asked questions, but was unwilling to receive answers. Let us take — said the Prediger — the 'children's catechism'. In the course of this the instructor asks, 'What are you?'

Q *A I am a human being.*
Q Do you feel it when I take hold of you?
A *I feel it well.*
Q What is this, is it not flesh?
A *Yes, that is flesh.*
Q All this flesh which you have is called the body. What is it called?
A *The body.*
Q How do you know when people have died?
A *They cannot speak, they cannot move anymore.*
Q Do you know why not?
A *I do not know why not.*

'Could he not answer these questions?' cried the Freiherr.

'It may be that he could, but the answers he gave in fact were not correct. A child of not quite ten years old, he insists that the body is not flesh, but the same stuff as the soul.'

'But this is only one instance —'

'I could give many others.'

'He has not yet learned —'

'He is dreaming away his opportunities. He will never become an acceptable member of Neudietendorf.'

The Freiherr asked whether not even one sign of moral grace had been detected in his son. The Prediger avoided a reply.

The mother, poor Auguste, who soon became sickly (although she outlived all but one of her eleven children) and seemed always to be looking for someone to whom to apologise, begged to be allowed to teach Fritz herself. But what could she have taught him? A little music perhaps. A tutor was hired from Leipzig.

6

Uncle Wilhelm

WHILE they were living at Oberwiederstadt, the Hardenbergs did not invite their neighbours, and did not accept their invitations, knowing that this might lead to worldliness. There was also the question of limited means. The Seven Years' War was expensive – Friedrich II was obliged to open a state lottery to pay for it – and for some of his loyal landholders, quite ruinous. In 1780 four of the smaller Hardenberg properties had to be sold, and at another one, Möckritz, there was an auction of the entire contents. Now it stood there without crockery, without curtains, without livestock. As far as the low horizon the fields lay uncultivated. At Oberwiederstadt itself, you saw through the narrow ancient windows row after row of empty dovecotes, and a *Gutshof* too vast to be filled, or even half-filled, which had once been the convent chapel. The main building was pitiable, with missing tiles, patched, weatherbeaten, stained with water which had run for years from the loosened guttering. The pasture was dry over the old plague tombstones.

The fields were starved. The cattle stood feeding at the bottom of the ditches, where it was damp and a little grass grew.

Smaller and much more agreeable was Schlöben-bei-Jena, to which the family sometimes made an expedition. At Schlöben, with its mill-stream and mossy oaks, 'the heart,' Auguste said tentatively, 'can find peace'. But Schlöben was in almost as much difficulty as the other properties. There is nothing peaceful, the Freiherr told her, about a refusal to extend credit.

As a member of the nobility, most ways of earning money were forbidden to the Freiherr, but he had the right to enter the service of his Prince. In 1784 (as soon as the existing Director had died) he was appointed Director of the Salt Mines of the Electorate of Saxony at Dürrenberg, Kösen and Artern, at a salary of 650 thaler and certain concessions of firewood. The Central Saline Offices were at Weissenfels, and in 1786 the Freiherr bought the house in the Kloster Gasse. It was not like Schlöben, but Auguste wept with relief, praying that her tears were not those of ingratitude, at leaving the chilly solitude and terribly out-of-date household arrangements of Oberwiederstadt. Weissenfels had two thousand inhabitants − two thousand living souls − brickyards, a prison, a poor-house, the old former palace, a pig-market, the river's traffic and the great clouds reflected in the shining reach, a bridge, a hospital, a Thursday market, drying-meadows and many, many shops, perhaps thirty. Although the Freifrau had no spending allowance of her own and had never been into a shop, indeed rarely left the house except on Sundays, she received a faltering glow, like an uncertain hour of winter sunshine, from the idea of there being so many things and so many people quite close at hand.

It was at Weissenfels that the Bernhard was born, in the bitter February of 1788. Fritz by then was nearly seventeen, and was not at Weissenfels on this occasion, but at his Uncle Wilhelm's, in Lucklum in the Duchy of Braunschweig-Wolfenbüttel. The boy had outgrown his tutor, who had to sit up late into the night reading mathematics and physiology in order to catch up with him. 'But this is not wonderful, after all,' the uncle wrote. 'Tutors are a poor-spirited class of men, and all this Herrnhuterei is nothing but hymn-singing and house-work, quite unsuitable for a von Hardenberg. Send Fritz, for a time at least, to live in my household. He is fifteen or sixteen, I don't know which, and must learn to under-stand wine, which he can't do at Weissenfels, where the grapes are only fit to make brandy and vinegar, and to find out what grown men talk about when they are in decent company.' The Freiherr was, as always, infuriated by his brother's remarks and still more by their tone. Wilhelm was ten years older than himself, and appeared to have been sent into the world primarily to irritate him. He was a person of great distinction − 'in his own eyes' the Freiherr added − Governor of the Saxon division of the German Order of Knighthood (Lucklum branch). Round his neck, on very many occasions, he wore the flashy Maltese cross of the order, which was also embroidered, in plush and braid, on his greatcoat. The Hardenberg children knew him as the 'Big Cross', and His Mightiness. He had never married, and was graciously hospitable not only to his fellow landowners but to musicians, politicians, and philosophers − those who should be seen round the table of a great man, to offer their opinions and to agree with his own.

After a stay of only a few months, Fritz was returned to his father at Weissenfels, taking with him a letter from his uncle.

Lucklum, October 1787

I am glad that Fritz has recovered himself and got back on to the straight path, from which I certainly shall never try to remove him again. My way of life here is pitched too high for his young head. He was much too spoiled, and saw too many strange new people, and it could not be helped if a great many things were said at my table which were not helpful or salutary for him to know . . .

The Freiherr wrote to his brother to thank him for his hospitality, and to regret that he could not thank him more. The white waistcoat, breeches and broad-cloth coat which had been made for Fritz by his uncle's tailor, apparently because those he had brought with him were not considered smart enough for the dinner-table, would now be sent to the Moravian Brethren for distribution to charity. There would be no occasion for him to wear them in Weissenfels, where they lived simply.

'Best of Fritzes, you were lucky,' said fourteen-year-old Erasmus.

'I am not sure about that,' said Fritz. 'Luck has its rules, if you can understand them, and then it is scarcely luck.'

'Yes, but every evening at dinner, to sit there while these important people amused themselves by giving you too much to drink, to have your glass filled up again and again with fine wines, I don't know what . . . What did they talk about?'

'Nature-philosophy, galvanism, animal magnetism and freemasonry,' said Fritz.

'I don't believe it. You drink wine to forget things like that. And then at night, when the pretty women come creaking on tiptoe up the stairs to find the young inno- cent, and tap at your door, *TRIUMPH!*'

'There were no women,' Fritz told him. 'I think per- haps my uncle did not invite any.'

'No women!' cried Erasmus. 'Who then did the washing?'

7

The Freiherr and the French Revolution

WERE things worse at Weissenfels when a letter from the Big Cross arrived, or when the Mother's elder brother, Captain August von Böltzig, happened to come to the house? Von Böltzig had fought in the same battalion as the Freiherr in the Seven Years' War, but had come to totally different conclusions. The King of Prussia, whom he admired without reservations, had supported total freedom in religious belief, and the Prussian army was notably fearless and morally upright. Must one then not conclude –

'I can see what you have in mind to say next,' said the Freiherr, his voice still just kept in check. 'You mean that you accept my reasoning,' said von Böltzig. 'You admit that there is no connection, or none that can be demonstrated, between religion and right conduct?'

'I accept that you, August von Böltzig, are a very great fool.' The Freifrau felt trapped between the two of them, like a powder of thinly-ground meal between the mill-stones. One of her night fears (she was a poor sleeper) was that her brother and the Uncle Wilhelm might arrive, unannounced, at the same time. What would she be able to do or say, to get decently rid of one of them? Large though the house was, she always found guests a difficulty. The bell rang, you heard the servants crossing the hall, everything was on top of you before you could pray for guidance.

In 1790, by which time the young Fritz had matriculated at the University of Jena, the forces of history itself seemed to take a hand against Auguste. But here her narrowness of mind was an advantage, in that she saw them as no more and no less important than the worn bed-linen, or her brother's godlessness. Like the damp river-breeze, which made the bones ache, the disturbances in France seemed to her no more than a device to infuriate her husband.

Breakfast at Weissenfels was taken in a frugal style. On the dining room stove, at six o'clock in the morning, there were ranks of earthenware coffee-pots, the coffee being partly made, for economy's sake, out of burnt carrot powder. On the table stood large thick cups and saucers and a mountain of white rolls. The family, still in their nightclothes, appeared in ones and twos and, like sleepwalkers, helped themselves from the capacious earthenware pots. Some of the coffee they drank, some they sucked in through pieces broken off from the white rolls. Anyone who had finished turned his or her cup upsidedown on the saucer, calling out decisively, '*Satt!*'

As the boys grew older, Auguste did not like them to linger in the dining room. 'What are you speaking of, young men?' Erasmus and Karl stood warming themselves, close to the stove. 'You know that your father does not like . . .'

'He will be quite happy with the Girondins,' said Karl.

'But Karl, these people may perhaps have new ideas. He does not like new ideas.'

In the January of 1793, Fritz arrived from Jena in the middle of the breakfast, in a blue cloth coat with immense brass buttons, patched across the shoulder-blades, and a round hat. 'I will change my clothes, and come and sit with you.'

'Have you brought a newspaper?' Erasmus asked. Fritz looked at his mother, and hesitated. 'I think so.' The Freiherr, on this occasion, was sitting in his place at the head of the table. He said, 'I think you must know whether you have brought a newspaper or not.' Fritz handed him a copy, many times folded, of the *Jenaer Allgemeine Zeitung*. The paper was still cold from the freezing journey, in Fritz's outside pocket, from Jena.

The Freiherr unfolded it and uncreased it, took out his spectacles and in front of his silent family bent his attention on the closely printed front page. At first he said, 'I don't understand what I am reading.'

'The convention have served a writ of accusation on Louis,' said Fritz courageously.

'Yes, I read those words, but they were altogether beyond me. They are going to bring a civil action against the legitimate king of France?'

'Yes, they accuse him of treason.'

'They have gone mad.'

The Freiherr sat for a moment, in monumental stillness, among the coffee-cups. Then he said, 'I shall not touch another newspaper until the French nation returns to its senses again.'

He left the room. '*Satt*! *Satt*! *Satt*!' shouted Erasmus, drumming on his saucer. 'The revolution is the ultimate event, no interpretation is possible, what is certain is that a republic is the way forward for all humanity.'

'It is possible to make the world new,' said Fritz, 'or rather to restore it to what it once was, for the golden age was certainly once a reality.'

'And the Bernhard is here, sitting under the table!' cried the Freifrau, openly weeping. 'He will have heard every word, and every word he hears he will repeat.'

'It is not worth listening to, I know it already,' said the Bernhard, emerging from the tablecloth's stiff folds. 'They will cut his head off, you will see.'

'He does not know what he is saying! The king is the father, the nation is his family.'

'When the golden age returns there will be no fathers,' murmured the Bernhard. 'What is he saying?' asked poor Auguste.

She was right, however, in believing that with the French Revolution her troubles would be greatly increased. Her husband had not absolutely forbidden the appearance of newspapers in the house, so that she would be able to say to herself, 'It is only that he wants not to catch sight of them at table, or in his study.' For some other way had to be devised by which he could satisfy his immense curiosity about the escapades of the French which meant – if she was to tell the truth – nothing to her whatsoever. At the Saline offices, she supposed, and at the club – the Literary and Scientific Athenaeum of Weissenfels – he would hear the topics of the day discussed, but she knew, with the insight of long habit, so much more reliable than love, that whatever had happened would not be real to him – that he would not be able to feel he truly possessed it until he had seen it on the grey pages of a daily newspaper. 'Another time, dear Fritz, when you give your greatcoat to the servants to be brushed, you could leave your newspaper showing, just a few inches.'

'Mother, after all these years you don't know my Father. He has said he will not read the paper, and he will not.'

'But Fritz, how will he inform himself? The Brethren

won't tell him anything, they don't speak to him of worldly matters.'

'*Weiss Gott!*' said Fritz. 'Osmosis, perhaps.'

8

In Jena

THE Freiherr thought it best for his eldest son to be educated in the German manner, at as many universities as possible: Jena for a year, Leipzig for a year, by which time Erasmus would be old enough to join him, then a year at Wittenberg to study law, so that he would be able, if occasion arose, to protect whatever property the family had left through the courts. He was also to begin on theology, and on the constitution of the Electorate of Saxony. Instead of these subjects, Fritz registered for history and philosophy.

As a result he attended on his very first morning in Jena a lecture by Johann Gottlieb Fichte. Fichte was speaking of the philosophy of Kant, which, fortunately, he had been able to improve upon greatly. Kant believed in the external world. Even though it is only known to us through our senses and our own experience, still, it is there. This, Fichte was saying, was nothing but an old man's weakness. We are all free to imagine what the world is like, and since we probably all imagine it differently, there is no reason at all to believe in the fixed reality of things.

Before Fichte's gooseberry eyes the students, who had the worst reputation for unruliness in Germany, cowered, transformed into frightened schoolboys. 'Gentlemen! withdraw into yourselves! Withdraw into your own mind!' Arrogant and drunken in their free time, they waited, submissive. Each unhooked the little penny inkwell on a spike from behind a lapel of his jacket. Some straightened up, some bowed themselves over, closing their eyes. A few trembled with eagerness. 'Gentlemen, let your thought be the wall.' All were intent. 'Have you thought the wall?' asked Fichte. 'Now, then, gentlemen, let your thought be *that* that thought the wall.'

Fichte was the son of a linen-weaver, and in politics a Jacobin. His voice carried without effort. 'The gentleman in the fourth seat from the left at the back, who has the air of being in discomfort . . .'

A wretched youth rose to his feet.

'Herr Professor, that is because the chairs in the lecture-rooms of Jena are made for those with short legs.'

'My appointment as Professor will not be confirmed until next May. You are permitted to ask one question.'

'Why . . . ?'

'Speak up!'

'Why do we imagine that the wall is as we see it, and not as something other?'

Fichte replied, 'We create the world not out of our imagination, but out of our sense of duty. We need the world so that we may have the greatest possible number of opportunities to do our duty. That is what justifies philosophy, and German philosophy in particular.'

Late into the windy lamp-lit autumn night Jena's students met to *fichtisieren*, to talk about Fichte and his system. They appeared to be driving themselves mad. At two o'clock in the morning Fritz suddenly stood still in the middle of the Unterer Markt, letting the others stagger on in ragged groups without him, and said aloud to the stars, 'I see the fault in Fichte's system. There is no place in it for love.'

'You are outside his house,' said a passing student, sitting down on the cobblestones. 'His house is 12a. 12a is where Professor Fichte lives.'

'He is not a Professor until May,' said Fritz. 'We can serenade him until then. We can sing beneath his window, "We know what is wrong with your system . . . There is no place in it, no place in it for love."'

There were lodgings of all sorts in Jena. Some of the very poor students were entitled to eat free, as a kind of scholarship. They chose their eating-house, and could have their dinner only there and only up to a certain amount, a frightening sight, since the inn-keepers hurried them on, in order to clear the tables, and they were obliged to cram and splutter, snatching at the chance, like fiends in hell, of the last permitted morsel. But every one of them, no matter how wretched, belonged to a *Landsmannschaft*, a fellowship of their own region, even if that was only a hometown and numberless acres of potatoes. In the evenings, groups of friends moved from pothouse to smoky pothouse, looking for other friends and then summoning them, in the name of their *Landsmannschaft*, to avenge some insult or discuss a fine point of Nature-philosophy, or to get drunk, or, if already drunk, then drunker.

Fritz could have lived at Schlöben, but it was two hours away. He lodged at first — since she charged him nothing — with his Aunt Johanna Elizabeth. Elizabeth complained that she saw very little of him. 'I had so much looked forward to having a poet at my table. I myself, when I was a young woman, composed verses.' But Fritz, that first winter, had to spend an undue amount of time with his history teacher, the celebrated Professor Schiller. 'Dear Aunt, he is ill, it is his chest, a weakness has set in, all his pupils are taking it in turns to nurse him.'

'Nephew, you haven't the slightest idea how to nurse anyone.'

'He is a very great man.'

'Well, they are the most difficult to nurse.'

The Professor of Medicine and principal doctor to the University, Hofrat Johann Stark, was called in. He was a follower, like most of his colleagues, of the Brownian system. Dr Brown, of Edinburgh, had cured a number of patients by refusing to let blood, and by recommending exercise, sufficient sex, and fresh air. But he held that to be alive was not a natural state, and to prevent immediate collapse the constitution must be held in perpetual balance by a series of stimuli, either jacking it up with alcohol, or damping it down with opium. Schiller, although himself a believer in Brownismus, would take neither, but propped himself up against the bedstead, calling on his students to get paper and ink and take down notes at his dictation: 'To what end does man study universal history?'

It was at this time, when Fritz was emptying the sick room chamberpots, and later, watching the Professor at length put a lean foot to the floor, that he was first described in a letter by the critic Friedrich Schlegel. Schlegel was writing to his much more successful, elder brother, August Wilhelm, a professor of literature and aesthetics. He was in triumph at having discovered someone of interest whom his brother did not know. 'Fate has put into my hands a young man, from whom everything may be expected, and he explained himself to me at once with fire – with indescribably much fire. He is thin and well-made, with a beautiful expression when he gets carried away. He talks three times as much, and as fast, as the rest of us. On the very first evening he told me that the golden age would return, and that there was nothing evil in the world. I don't know if he is still of the same opinion. His name is von Hardenberg.'

9

An Incident in Student Life

'I shall not forget it,' said Fritz, thinking of an early morning in May, towards the end of his year in Jena. His Aunt Johanna had died of pneumonia in the bitter spring winds which Professor Schiller had just survived, and Fritz had lodgings in Schustergasse 4 (second staircase up), which he shared with a distant cousin – but where was this cousin when Fritz woke up, having been dragged out of bed half naked?

'He and some others are in the students' prison,' said the visitor, not a friend, hardly an acquaintance. 'You all went out together yesterday evening –'

'Very good, but in that case why am I not in the Black Hole along with them?'

'You have a better sense of direction than they have, and you were not arrested. But now you must come with me, you're needed.'

Fritz opened his eyes wide. 'You are Diethelm. You are a medical student.'

'No, my name is Dietmahler. Get up, put on your shirt and jacket.'

'I have seen you in Professor Fichte's lectures,' said Fritz, grasping the water-jug. 'And you wrote a song: it begins "In Distant Lands the Maiden . . ."'

'I am fond of music. Come, we have not much time.'

Jena being in a bare hollow, at the foot of a cliff, you can only get out of it by walking steadily uphill. It was still only four o'clock in the morning, but as they tramped up in the direction of Galgenberg they could feel the whole stagnant little town beginning to steam in its early summer heat. The sky was not quite light, but seemed to be thinning and lifting into a cloudless pallor. Fritz had begun to understand. There must have been a quarrel last night, or at least a dispute, about which he remembered nothing. If a duel was to be fought, which in itself was a prison offence, you needed a doctor, or since no respectable doctor could be asked to attend, then a medical student.

'Am I the referee?' Fritz asked.

'Yes.'

The referee in a Jena duel had to decide the impossible. The students' sword, the *Schläger*, was triangular, but rounded towards the point, so that only a deep three-cornered wound was allowed to score.

'Who has challenged who?' he asked.

'Joseph Beck. He sent me a note to say he must fight,

who or why he did not say. Only the time and place.'

'I don't know him.'

'Your rooms were the nearest.'

'I am glad he has so true a friend.'

They were now above the mist level, where the dew was beginning to dry, and turned through a gate into a field which had been cleared of young turnips. Two students were hard at it, with flapping shirt-tails, attacking each other without grace or skill on the hardened, broken, yellowish ground.

'They started without us,' said Dietmahler. 'Run!'

As they crossed the field one of the duellists cut and ran for it to a gate in the other direction. His opponent left standing, dropped his *Schläger*, then fell himself, with his right hand masked in blood, perhaps cut off.

'No, only two fingers,' said Dietmahler, urgently bending down to the earth, where weeds and coarse grass were already beginning to sprout. He picked up the fingers, red and wet as if skinned, one of them the top joint only, one with a gold ring.

'Put them in your mouth,' said Dietmahler. 'If they are kept warm I can perhaps sew them back on our return.'

Fritz was not likely to forget the sensation of the one and a half fingers and the heavy ring, smooth and hard while they were yielding, in his mouth.

'All Nature is one,' he told himself.

At the same time (his own common sense told him to do this, without instructions from Dietmahler) he gripped the blubbering and spouting Joseph Beck under the right elbow, to hold up his forearm and keep the veins at the back of the hand empty. Meanwhile the whole sky, from one hilltop horizon to the other, was filled with light, and the larks began to go up. In the next meadow hares had stolen out to feed.

'As long as his thumb is saved, his hand may still be of use to him,' Dietmahler remarked. Fritz, with no way of swallowing his own saliva, mixed with earth and blood, thought, 'This is all of interest to him as a doctor. But, as a philosopher, it doesn't help me.'

They returned to Jena in a woodcutter's cart which was providentially going downhill. Even the woodcutter, who normally paid no attention to anything that did not concern him directly, was impressed by the cries and groans of poor Beck. 'The gentleman is perhaps a singer?'

'Drive straight to the Anatomy Theatre,' Dietmahler told him. 'If it is open, I may be able to find needles and gut.'

It was too early to buy either schnaps or opium, though Dietmahler, who was also a disciple of Brownismus, was impatient to pour quantities of both down his patient.

10

A Question of Money

IN the Michaelmas of 1791 Fritz began the second stage of his university education, at Leipzig. He was nineteen, and Leipzig, with fifty thousand inhabitants, was the largest town he had ever lived in. He found it impossible to manage on the allowance that could be spared for him.

'I must speak to Father,' he told Erasmus.

'He will be displeased.'

'How many people are pleased when they are asked for money?'

'What have you done with it, Fritz?'

'Well, I have spent what I had on the necessities of life. There is the soul, and there is the flesh. But the old one too, when he was a student, must have had these necessities.'

'That would be before he was awakened,' said Erasmus gloomily. 'You cannot expect sympathy from him now. Nineteen years should have taught you that much.'

On his next return to Weissenfels, Fritz said: 'Father, I am young, and, speaking with due respect, I cannot live like an old man. I have kept myself under extreme restraint in Leipzig, I have ordered one pair of shoes only since I have been there. I have grown my hair long to avoid expense at the barber. In the evening I eat only bread . . .'

'In what respects do you find that you cannot live like an old man?' asked the Freiherr.

Fritz shifted his ground.

'Father, there is not a student in Leipzig who does not owe money. I cannot manage on what you allow me at the moment. There are six of us still at home, I know, but we still have estates at Oberwiederstadt, and at Schlöben.'

'Did you think I had forgotten them?' asked the Freiherr.

He passed his hand over his face.

'Go to Oberwiederstadt, and see Steinbrecher. I will give you a letter to him.'

Steinbrecher was the revenue steward.

'But isn't he at Schlöben?'

'He deals now with all our properties. This month he is at Oberwiederstadt.'

Fritz took a place in the diligence, which left the Stag in Weissenfels at four in the morning, and went by way of Halle and Eisleben. The German diligence was the slowest in Europe, since all the luggage, which was loaded onto a kind of creaking extension of the floor extending over the back axle, had to be unloaded and re-loaded every time a passenger got in or out. While the conductor supervised this work the driver fed himself and his horses, on loaves of coarse brown bread.

At the Black Boy at Eisleben a farm servant was sitting on the bench outside, waiting for him.

'*Grüss dich*, Joseph,' said Fritz, remembering him from seven years back. 'Let us go into the grocer's and take a glass of schnaps.' In Saxony the inns were not allowed to sell spirits.

'I should be sorry to see your father's son diverting himself in such a way,' Joseph replied.

'But, Joseph, I was hoping to divert *you*.' This, it was clear, was not possible. The inn provided horses, and in silence they rode to Oberwiederstadt.

The revenue steward was waiting for them, although by now it was dark. Fritz presented his father's letter, and waited for him to read it through twice. Then, feeling the awkwardness of silence, he said, 'Herr Revenue Steward, I think my Father has commissioned you to give me some money.'

Steinbrecher took off his spectacles.

'Young Freiherr, there is no money.'

'He sent me a long way to be told that.'

'I imagine that he wanted you to remember it.'

11

A Disagreement

FRITZ walked the thirty-two miles back to Weissenfels. When he reached the Kloster Gasse his father had returned from the offices of the Salt Mines Administration, but he was not alone.

'His Highmindedness, the Uncle Wilhelm, is here,' Sidonie told him. 'The Big Cross himself. They are discussing your affairs. How did you get on with Steinbrecher? I'll tell you what I think, it's this: if some people were not older than others, and young people were as rich as old ones—'

'But, Sidonie, I really believe now that we are much poorer even than we thought.'

'You don't ask me what I believe,' said Sidonie. 'I am here in the house, I have more opportunity to think about it than you do.'

'It depends on all of us now, but on myself in particular —' Fritz began, but the Bernhard, who had made his appearance, interrupted: 'I am the chief sufferer. When the Big Cross is here, my mother brings me forward, believing that I am his favourite. In fact he dislikes children, and myself in particular.'

'He will expect better wine and more company than we usually have,' said Sidonie. 'He mentioned that, you know, the last time he honoured us with a visit.'

'Last time I was called upon to recite,' the Bernhard continued, 'my uncle shouted: "For what reason has he been taught such idiocies?"'

'My mother is not in the salon,' said Sidonie. 'What shall I tell her to do?'

'Nothing,' said Karl, who was lying at ease on the only sofa. His position was unassailable. In a week he was off to begin his military training as a cadet with a regiment of carabiniers in the service of the Elector of Saxony. He was therefore approved of by his Uncle Wilhelm, even though he had never been invited to Lucklum. Fritz appeared not to be listening. Some urgency, some private resolution seemed to possess him. Sidonie had not noticed it when he first walked in, she had perhaps been too pleased to see him, but now it was unmistakable, as though he had brought an embarrassing stranger in with him, who was waiting for the moment of introduction.

In the reception room the Big Cross did not take a chair, but walked rapidly up and down, displaying each time he turned back into the room the dazzling emblem on his dark blue cloak. The Freiherr, tired after a day of disputes at the Inspectorate, sat in his roomy elbow-chair, thinking that if his brother did not take off his outer garment, there was some hope that he would soon go. 'But where is your wife, where is Auguste?' enquired Wilhelm.

'I don't imagine she will appear this afternoon.'

'Why is that? She need not fear me, I am not a spook.'

'She needs rest, she is delicate.'

'If a woman keeps working, she will find she is never tired.'

'You have never married, Wilhelm. But here, at least, is Friedrich.' Fritz, pale as clay, came into the salon, and after greeting his father and his uncle not quite attentively enough began at full pitch.

'I want to tell you that I have decided what I am to do with my life. It came to me on the journey back from Oberwiederstadt.'

'How fortunate that I am here,' said the Big Cross, 'just when my advice is most needed.'

'During my studies at Jena and now at Leipzig you, Uncle, have taken it amiss because I preferred philosophy and history to law, and you Father, have been offended when I said that even law would be preferable to theology. But now I want both of you to put these anxieties away from you — to blow them away, as if they were dust from the earth. I see now that my duty is to be a soldier. Everything points to it. In that way I shall cost you nothing. And I know now that I need discipline. I have romantic tendencies. In a barracks these will be corrected by the practical, unromantic duties of my daily life — the shit house, the fever ward, the route march, foot inspection. Later, when I see action, I shall have nothing to fear, because life, after all, is a goal, not a means. I have it in mind to apply to the Cuirassiers of the Elector's Guard.'

'*Scheisskerl*, shut your muzzle!' bellowed the Big Cross.

'That is not the way to address my son, or any decent man's son,' said the Freiherr. 'But it's true that he's talking like an idiot.'

'But Karl —' Fritz broke in.

'— is a smart young fellow, anxious to start life on his own account,' the Uncle cried. 'Whereas you! — The Cuirassiers! — I have heard you say at my own table, when you were the age that Karl is now, that life would be better if it were a dream, and that perhaps it will become one. Where is your practical ability? You've never even seen a man wounded!'

Fritz left the room. 'Whatever you have been talking about, you have put things much too strongly,' said Sidonie, coming past with two of the servants carrying coffee and bread and butter, which the Uncle, in disgust, waved away from a distance.

'At least they are agreed,' said Fritz. 'They are at one in thinking me incapable, and possibly a coward.'

Sidonie pressed his elbow in sympathy. But through the open doors of the salon the Uncle and the Father could be seen to turn towards each other in furious confrontation.

'Leave your son's concerns to me. You know absolutely nothing of these matters.'

'You forget that I served seven years in the Hanoverian Legion,' cried the Freiherr.

'But without acquiring the slightest military competence.'

Karl and Sidonie took the dejected Fritz into the garden, and down to the orchard. 'We're going to have pears and plums innumerable this year,' said Sidonie. 'Wherever did you get such a stupid idea? Why should you think you would ever make a soldier?'

'Where is your sense?' added Karl.

'I don't know. Tell me, Karl, what makes a man a soldier?'

'I, myself, wanted to enter the service of my Prince. I also wanted to get away from home,' said Karl.

'Won't you miss us, Karl?' asked Sidonie.

'I cannot afford to think about that sort of thing. I am of more use to you all, in any case, out in the world. And you, Sido, will soon be married, and forget about your brothers.'

'Never!' cried Sidonie.

12

The Sense of Immortality

ONCE he had got rid of the Uncle and his travelling entourage of body-servants and cooks, who had been infesting the kitchen quarters, Freiherr von Hardenberg summoned his eldest son and told him that after his year at Leipzig and a further year at Wittenberg to study chemistry, geology and law he would be ready to take his first steps as a trainee clerk in the Directorate of Salt Mines. Erasmus would be sent from Leipzig to Hubertusberg, where he would enrol in the School of Forestry, a wholesome, open-air life for which so far he had shown no inclination whatsoever. Karl had already seen action, at the age of sixteen. He had been with his regiment when the French were driven out of Mainz. He expected to come home frequently. It was not at all difficult to get army leave. Officers on leave were not paid, so that until they reported back, the regiment was able to save money.

If Fritz sometimes took the diligence, or walked long distances, it was because he rarely had a decent horse to ride. If ever he managed to hire or borrow one, he noted it down in his diary. His own horse, known only as the Gaul (the Crock), he could remember at Oberwiederstadt, although he had been too young to ride him until they moved to Weissenfels. How old was the Gaul? Age had brought him cunning, rather than wisdom, and he had arrived with his master at an elaborate creaturely bargain as to place and time – when he might slow down, when he might stop, when consent to go on. Fritz did not disturb himself about his own appearance, or about the shabbiness of his horse, as long as they could get from one point to another.

From the age of seventeen he had been in almost perpetual motion, or the Gaul's unhurried version of it, back and forth, though not over a wide area. His life was lived in the 'golden hollow' in the Holy Roman Empire, bounded by the Harz Mountains and the deep forest, crossed by rivers – the Saale, the Unstrut, the Helme, the Elster, the Wipper – proceeding in gracious though seemingly quite unnecessary bends and sweeps past mine-workings, salt-houses, timber-mills, waterside inns where the customers sat placidly hour after hour, waiting for the fish to be caught from the river and broiled. Scores of miles of rolling country, uncomplainingly bringing forth potatoes and turnips and the great whiteheart pickling cabbages which had to be sliced with a saw, lay between hometown and hometown, each with its ownness, but also its welcome likeness to the last one. The hometowns were reassuring to the traveller, who fixed his sights from a distance on the wooden roof of the old church, the cupola of the new one, and came at length to the streets of small houses drawn up in order, each with its pig sty, its prune oven and bread oven and sometimes its wooden garden-house, where the master, in the cool of the evening, sat smoking in total blankness of mind, under a carved motto: ALL HAPPINESS IS HERE or CONTENTMENT IS WEALTH. Sometimes, though not often, a woman, also, found time to sit in the garden-house.

When Fritz rode back southwards from Wittenberg at the end of his year's studies, it was a day in a thousand, crystal-clear, heavenly blue. They were just beginning the potato-lifting, with which he had so often helped, willingly enough, as a child with the Brethren at Neudiet-endorf.

Between Rippach and Lützen he stopped where a stream crossed the road, to let the Gaul have a drink, although the horse usually had to wait for this until the end of the day. As Fritz loosened the girths, the Gaul breathed in enormously, as though he had scarcely known until that moment what air was. Fritz's valise, tied to the crupper, rose and fell with a sound like a drum on his broad quarters. Then, deflating little by little, he lowered his head to the water to find the warmest and muddiest part, sank his jaws to a line just below the nostrils, and began to drink with an alarming energy which he had never displayed on the journey from Wittenberg.

Fritz sat by the empty roadside, on the damp Saxon earth which he loved, and with nothing in view except a convoy of potato-wagons and the line of alders which marked the course of the Elster. His education was now almost at an end. What had he learned? Fichtean philosophy, geology, chemistry, combinatorial mathematics, Saxon commercial law. One of his greatest friends in Jena, the physicist Johann Wilhelm Ritter, had tried to show him that the ultimate explanation of life was galvanism, and that every exchange of energy between the mind and the body must be accompanied by an electric charge. Electricity was sometimes visible as light, but not all light was visible, indeed most of it was not. 'We must never judge by what we see.' Ritter was almost penniless. He had never attended a university, never in fact been to school. A glass of wine was immeasurable encouragement to him. After that, lying in his wretched lodgings, he could see the laws of electricity written in cloudy hieroglyphs on the whole surface of the universe, and on the face of the waters, where the Holy Spirit still moved.

– My teachers did not agree with each other, my friends did not agree with my teachers, Fritz thought, but that is only on a superficial level, they were men of intellect and passion, let me believe in them all.

The children of large families hardly ever learn to talk to themselves aloud, that is one of the arts of solitude, but they often keep diaries. Fritz took out his pocket journal. Certain words came readily to him – *weaknesses, faults, urges, striving for fame, striving against the crushing, wretched, bourgeois conditions of everyday life, youth, despair*. Then he wrote, 'But I have, I can't deny it, a certain inexpressible sense of immortality.'

13

The Just Family

'YOU have heard me speak of Kreisamtmann Coelestin
Just of Tennstedt,' said the Freiherr. Fritz thought that
he had. 'He is of course the local presiding magistrate,
but also, which is not always the case, supervisor of the
tax collection for his district. I have arranged for you to
study with him at Tennstedt in order to learn administration and practical office management, of which you
know nothing.' Fritz asked if he should take lodgings.
'No, you will lodge with the Justs themselves. The Kreisamtmann has a niece, Karoline, a very steady young
woman who keeps house for him, and in addition he
has married, at the age of forty-six, the widow of Christian
Nürnberger, the late Professor of Anatomy and Botany
at Wittenberg. Very likely you may have met her there,
during the past year.'

In the University towns it might be different, but no
woman in Weissenfels, Tennstedt, Grüningen or Langensalza tried to look younger than they were or knew of

any way of doing so. They accepted what the years sent.

Karoline Just saw, when she looked in her glass, the face of a woman of twenty-seven, uniformly smooth and pale, with noticeably dark eyebrows. She had been housekeeping for her Uncle Coelestin Just at his house in Tennstedt for four years. It had not been thought that her uncle would ever marry, but only six months ago he had done so. 'My dear, you will be glad for me and for yourself,' he had said. 'If at any time now the question arises of your making a home of your own, you will be able to be sure that you are not deserting me.'

'The question has not arisen,' said Karoline.

That Karoline had nowhere else to go, except back to Merseburg (where her father was Pronotary of the Cathedral Seminary) did not strike Just as a difficulty. In either place she was truly welcome. Meanwhile he congratulated himself that his Rahel was not only that most eligible of German women, a Professor's widow, but also, at thirty-nine, most likely past the age of child-bearing. The three of them could live peaceably together without unwelcome change or disturbance.

In Tennstedt they said — Now he has two women under one roof. Well, there's a proverb ... Who, then, is going to give the orders and spend the Kreisamtmann's money? — About the expected lodger — expected because the servants were talking about him, and because an extra bedstead had been purchased – they knew that he was said to be twenty-two years of age.

At the Universities the professors often arranged for their daughters to marry their likeliest pupil. Everywhere master carpenters, printers and bakers were satisfied when a daughter, or a niece, married one of their apprentices. The Kreisamtmann was neither a professor nor a skilled craftsman, he was a magistrate and an area tax-inspector, and such an arrangement might never have occurred to him, but now that he was a married man, they said, he had someone else to do the thinking for him.

Fritz arrived on foot, a day after he was expected, and at a time when Coelestin Just was at his office. 'The Long-Expected is here,' said Rahel to Karoline. She herself remembered him very well from Wittenberg, but was distressed to see him so dishevelled. 'You find the exercise healthy, Hardenberg?' she asked anxiously as she brought him into the house. Fritz looked at her vaguely, but with a radiant smile. 'I don't know, Frau Rahel. I hadn't thought about it, but I will think about it.' Once in the parlour, he looked round him as though at a revelation. 'It is beautiful, beautiful.'

'It's not beautiful at all,' said Rahel. 'You are more than welcome here, I hope that you will learn a great deal and you are free, of course, to form whatever opinions you like, but this parlour is not beautiful.'

Fritz continued to gaze around him.

'This is my niece by marriage, Karoline Just.'

Karoline was wearing her shawl and housekeeping apron.

'You are beautiful, gracious Fräulein,' said Fritz.

'We expected you yesterday,' said Rahel, dryly, 'but you see, we are patient people.' When Karoline had gone out, as she very soon did, to the kitchen, she added, 'I am going to take the privilege of someone who met you so often when you were a student, and welcomed you, you remember, to our Shakespeare evenings, and tell you that you ought not to speak to Karoline quite like that. You did not mean it, and she is not used to it.'

'But I did mean it,' said Fritz. 'When I came into your home, everything, the wine-decanter, the tea, the sugar, the chairs, the dark green tablecloth with its abundant fringe, everything was illuminated.'

'They are as usual. I did not buy this furniture myself, but –'

Fritz tried to explain that he had seen not their everyday, but their spiritual selves. He could not tell when these transfigurations would come to him. When the moment came it was as the whole world would be when body at last became subservient to soul.

Rahel saw that, whatever else, young Hardenberg was serious. She allowed herself to wonder whether he was obliged, on medical advice, to take much opium? For toothache, of course, everyone had to take it, she did not mean that. But she soon found out that he took at most thirty drops at bedtime as a sedative, if his mind was too active – only half the dose, in fact, that she took herself for a woman's usual aches and pains.

14

Fritz at Tennstedt

Fritz's luggage arrived a day later on the diligence. It consisted largely of books. Here were the hundred and thirty-three necessary titles, the earlier ones mostly poetry, plays and folktales, later on the study of plants, minerals, medicine, anatomy, theories of heat, sound and electricity, Mathematics, the Analysis of Infinite Numbers. They are all one, said Fritz aloud, warming his hands over a candle in his cold attic bedroom at Tennstedt. All human knowledge is one. Mathematics is the linking principle, just as Ritter told me that electricity is the link between body and mind. Mathematics is human reason itself in a form everyone can recognise. Why should poetry, reason and religion not be higher forms of Mathematics? All that is needed is a grammar of their common language. And if all knowledge was to be expressed through symbols, then he must set to work to write down every possible way the operation could be performed.

'*Triumph!*' exclaimed Fritz in his icy room (but he had never in his life – nor had anyone he knew – worked or slept in a room that was not exceedingly cold).

His second load of books began with Franz Ludwig Cancrinus' *Foundations of Mining and Saltworks*, Volume 1. Part 1: In What Mineralogy Consists. Part 2: In What the Art of Experiment Consists. Part 3: In What the Specification of Aboveground Earth Consists. Part 4: In What the Specification of Belowground Earth Consists. Part 5: In What the Art of Mine Construction Consists. Part 6: In What Arithmetic, Geometry and Ordinary Trigonometry Consists. Part 7, Section 1: In What Mechanics, Hydrostatics, Aerometrics and Hydraulics Consists, Section 2: In What the Construction of Mountain Machinery Consists. Part 8, Section 1: In What the Smelting and Precipitation of Metals from Ore Consists, Section 2: In What the Smelting of Half-metals Consists, Section 3: In What the Preparation of Sulphur Consists. Part 9, Section 1: In What the Examination of Salt and the Geological Description of Salt-Bearing Mountains Consists, Section 2: In What the Art of Salt-Boiling and the Construction of New Saltworks Consists. Volume 2, What is Understood by Mining and Salt Law.

The servants reported to Rahel that the young Freiherr was talking aloud to himself in his room. 'He goes up there immediately after breakfast,' Rahel told her husband, 'and you have seen that he also studies after dinner.' Just asked Karoline whether they could not have a little music one evening, as a relaxation. 'You must take pity', he suggested, 'on the unfortunate young man.'

'I know nothing about his trouble,' said Karoline. She found herself very busy with the work of the forewinter – sausage-making, beating flax for the winter spinning, killing the geese (who had already been plucked alive twice) for their third and last crop of down. After this it was necessary to eat baked goose for a week. But she took her place that evening in the parlour when Fritz, appealed to by Rahel, came downstairs, carrying a book – he had been persuaded to read aloud to them – or no, it was not a book, but a folder of manuscripts.

'You must not think that this was written to anyone in particular. I was at Jena. I was younger than I am now.

> *Accept my book, accept my little rhymes,*
> *Care for them if you can and let them go*
> *Do you want more? My heart, perhaps, my life?*
> *Those you had long ago.'*

He looked up – 'That would be very suitable to copy out in a young lady's album,' said Rahel. 'I'm afraid however we don't have anything of the sort in the house.'

Fritz tore the sheet of paper in half. Karoline put down the pillow-case she was mending. 'Please read more, read on.' Her Uncle Coelestin looked quietly at the glow from the stove, whose doors were slightly ajar. He had been told that young Hardenberg was a poet, but had only just realised that he intended to read his verses aloud. He could not pretend to be a judge of them. Singing was a different matter. Like everyone else he knew, Just sang himself, belonged to two singing clubs, and listened to singing indoors in winter and in summer in the open air, the woods, the mountains and the streets. Yes, and a friend of Karoline's, a high soprano, had possessed such a beautiful voice that at her wedding dinner, when all the notables of Tennstedt were present, Coelestin himself had been cajoled into appearing as an old bird-seller, with an armful of empty cages painted to represent gold, and into singing a comical country song, imploring the bride-groom 'not to take away their nightingale'. Yes, that was Else Wangel, only three years ago, three years since her wedding, and she was broad enough nowadays to fill a doorway.

Karoline was speaking to him reproachfully. 'Why are you talking of Else Wangel?'

'My dear, I did not know I was speaking aloud. All of you must pardon an old man.'

Just was forty-six. The melancholy of approaching mortality had been one of his reasons, first, for sending for his niece, then, in good time, for his marriage.

'Uncle, you have not been listening, you understood nothing.'

15

Justen

KAROLINE was in charge (Rahel having divided up the responsibilities with watchful tact) of the household accounts, which included collecting Fritz's weekly payment for board and lodging, also for stabling the Gaul, who had arrived from Weissenfels. On the very first Saturday, however, there was confusion. 'Fräulein Karoline, my father's cashier is due at Tennstedt to bring me my allowance from now until the end of November, but he has perhaps made a mistake and gone straight to Oberwiederstadt. I shall have to ask you I am afraid to wait for what is owing.'

'I don't think we can wait,' Karoline told him, 'but I will make it up, for the time being, from the housekeeping.' She had changed colour – which she scarcely ever did – at the idea of his embarrassment. 'How will he manage?' she asked Rahel. Rahel said, 'I dare say that in spite of attending three universities he has not been taught how to manage. He is the eldest son, and has not been protected from himself.'

Although the cashier arrived the next day, Karoline felt as if she had made some kind of a stand, but in reality she had no defences against Hardenberg, because, from the evening of the poetry-reading onwards he asked so much from her. He gave her his entire confidence, he laid the weight of it upon her. She was his friend — Karoline did not contradict this — and although he could live without love, he told her, he could not live without friendship. All was confessed, he talked perpetually. Neither the sewing nor the forewinter sausage-chopping deterred him. As she chopped, Karoline learned that the world is tending day by day not towards destruction, but towards infinity. She was told where Fichte's philosophy fell short, and that Hardenberg had a demon of a little brother of whom he was fond, and a monstrous uncle who disputed with his father, but then, so did they all.

'Your mother also?'

'No, no.'

'I am sorry you are not happy at home,' said Karoline.

Fritz was startled. 'I have given you the wrong idea, there is love in our home, we would give our lives for each other.'

His mother was young enough too, he added, to bear more children; it was his absolute duty to start earning as soon as possible. Then he returned to the subject of Fichte, fetching his lecture notes to show to Karoline — page after page of triadic patterns. 'Yes, these are some of Fichte's triads, but I will tell you what has suddenly struck me since I came to Tennstedt. You might look at them as representing the two of us. You are the thesis, tranquil, pale, finite, self-contained. I am the antithesis, uneasy, contradictory, passionate, reaching out beyond myself. Now we must question whether the synthesis will be harmony between us or whether it will lead to a new impossibility which we have never dreamed of.'

Karoline replied that she did not dream very much.

About Dr Brown, whom he spoke of next, she did know something, but she had not realised that Brownismus was an improvement on all previous medical systems, or that Dr Brown himself had lectured with a glass of whisky and a glass of laudanum in front of him, sipping from each in turn, to demonstrate the perfect balance. She did not even know what whisky was.

Fritz also told her that women are children of nature, so that nature, in a sense, is their art. 'Karoline, you must read *Wilhelm Meister*.'

'Of course I have read *Wilhelm Meister*,' she said.

Fritz was disconcerted for a few seconds, so that she had time to add, 'I found Mignon very irritating.'

'She is only a child,' cried Fritz, 'a spirit, or a spirit-seer, more than a child. She dies because the world is not holy enough to contain her.'

'She dies because Goethe couldn't think what to do

with her next. If he had made her marry Wilhelm Meister, that would have served both of them right.'

'You are very severe in your judgments,' said Fritz. He sat down to write a few verses on the subject. Karoline, with the kitchen-maid, was putting lengths of string through dried rings of apple. 'But Hardenberg, you have written about my eyebrows!'

> *Karoline Just has dark eyebrows*
> *And from the movements of her eyebrows*
> *I can gather good advice.*

'I shall give you a pet-name,' he said. 'You haven't got one?' Most Carolines and Karolines (and it was the commonest name in North Germany) were called Line, Lili, Lollie or Karolinchen. She shook her head. 'No, I have never had one.'

'I shall call you Justen,' he said.

16

The Jena Circle

TENNSTEDT had the advantage, from Just's point of view, of being over fifty miles from Jena. Young Hardenberg still had many friendships there, but, in Just's opinion, would be better off without them. For example, the physicist Johann Wilhelm Ritter — if that was what he was — should probably be committed, for his own good, to an asylum. But Ritter was an innocent. What struck Just in particular was the behaviour of the Jena women. Friedrich Schlegel, one of Hardenberg's earliest friends, was a great admirer of his brother August's wife, Caroline. This same wife had been the lover of George Forster, the librarian. Forster's wife Thérèse had left him for a journalist, complaining that when their baby died of smallpox, Forster had not consoled her but had simply 'taken strenuous steps to replace it'. Again, Friedrich Schlegel lived with a woman ten years older than himself. She was Dorothea, daughter of the philosopher Moses Mendelssohn, a kind and motherly woman, apparently, but she had a husband already, a banker, whose name Just couldn't remember. Whoever he was, he was well out of it.

They were all intelligent, all revolutionaries, but since each of them had a different plan, none of it would come to anything. They talked continually of going to Prussia, to Berlin, but they stayed in Jena. As Just saw it, this was because Jena was so much cheaper.

To the Jena circle Fritz was a kind of phenomenon, a country boy, perhaps still growing, capable in his enthusiasm of breaking things, tall and awkward. Friedrich Schlegel stuck to it that he was a genius. 'You must see him,' they told their acquaintances. 'Whatever you read of Hardenberg's you won't understand him nearly as well as if you take tea with him once.'

'When you write to him,' said the wild Caroline Schlegel to her sister-in-law Dorothea, 'tell him to come at once, and we will all *fichtisieren* and symphilosophise and *sympoetisieren* until the dawn breaks.'

'Yes,' said Dorothea, 'we must have the whole congregation together again in my front sitting room. I shall not be content until I see this. But in any case, why is our Hardenberg dragging round like a clerk under the orders of some tedious Kreisamtmann?'

'Oh, but the Kreisamtmann has a niece,' said Caroline.

'How old is she?' asked Dorothea.

17

What is the Meaning?

Now that the Gaul was in the Justs' stable, Fritz would be able to accompany the Kreisamtmann on circuit. There he was to act as his legal clerk, and to pick up business methods, as his father had specified, as he went.

In spite of his sober clothes, bought at second hand, Fritz did not look quite right, not quite like a clerk of any kind, and the Gaul also struck a jarring note. But the Kreisamtmann, from the moment he first saw Fritz, had taken him to his heart. The only precaution he thought necessary before they set out together on official business was to ask him whether he still felt as Just understood he once had about the sequence of events in France?

'The Revolution in France has not produced the effects once hoped for,' was how he put it to Fritz. 'It has not resulted in a golden age.'

'No, they've made a butcher's shop of it, I grant you that,' said Fritz. 'But the spirit of the Revolution, as we first heard of it, as it first came to us, could be preserved here in Germany. It could be transferred to the world of the imagination, and administered by poets.'

'It seems to me,' said Just, 'that as soon as you are settled into your profession, you would be well advised to take up politics.'

'Politics are the last thing that we need. This at least I learned with the Brethren at Neudietendorf. The state should be one family, bound by love.'

'That does not sound much like Prussia,' said the Kreis-amtmann.

To the Freiherr von Hardenberg he wrote that the whole relationship between himself and the son who had been entrusted to him was extremely successful. Friedrich was showing much application. Who would have guessed that he, the poet, would spare no pains to turn himself into a businessman, to do the same piece of work two or three times over, to go over the resemblances and differences in the words of newspaper articles about business matters so as to be sure he had judged them correctly, and all this as diligently as he read his poetry, science and philosophy. 'Of course, your son learns very quickly, twice as fast as other earthly mortals.'

'It is a curious thing that although I am supposed to be instructing him,' Just's letter went on, 'and *am* instructing him, he is teaching *me* even more, matters to which I never paid attention before, and in the process I am losing the narrow-mindedness of an old man. He has advised me to read *Robinson Crusoe* and *Wilhelm Meister*. I told him that up till this time I had never felt the least temptation to read a work of fiction.'

'What are these matters,' the Freiherr wrote back to him, 'to which you never paid attention before? Be good enough to give me one example.' Just replied that Fritz Hardenberg had spoken to him of a fable, which he had found, so far as Just could remember, in the works of the Dutch philosopher Franz Hemsterhuis – it had been about the problem of universal language, a time when plants, stars and stones talked on equal terms with animals and with man. For example, the sun communicates with the stone as it warms it. Once we knew the words of this language, and we shall do so again, since history always repeats itself. '– I told him, that is of course always a possibility, if God disposes.'

The Freiherr replied that his son would not need a different language from German to conduct his duties as a future salt mine inspector.

Since winter often left the roads impassable, Coelestin Just and his probationary clerk did as much of their travelling as possible before the end of the forewinter. 'But there is something else which I have written and which I want to read to you while I still have time,' Fritz told Karoline. 'It will not truly exist until you have heard it.'

'Is it then poetry?'

'It is poetry, but not verse.'

'Then it is a story?' asked Karoline, who dreaded the reappearance of Fichte's triads.

'It is the beginning of a story.'

'Well, we will wait until my Aunt Rahel comes back from the evening service.'

'No, it is for you only,' said Fritz.

'His father and mother were already in bed and asleep, the clock on the wall ticked with a monotonous beat, the wind whistled outside the rattling window-pane. From time to time the room grew brighter when the moonlight shone in. The young man lay restlessly on his bed and remembered the stranger and his stories. "It was not the thought of the treasure which stirred up such unspeakable longings in me," he said to himself. "I have no craving to be rich, but I long to see the blue flower. It lies incessantly at my heart, and I can imagine and think about nothing else. Never did I feel like this before. It is as if until now I had been dreaming, or as if sleep had carried me into another world. For in the world I used to live in, who would have troubled himself about flowers? Such a wild passion for a flower was never heard of there. But where could this stranger have come from? None of us had ever seen such a man before. And yet I don't know how it was that I alone was truly caught and held by what he told us. Everyone else heard what I did, and yet none of them paid him serious attention."'

'Have you read this to anyone else, Hardenberg?'

'Never to anyone else. How could I? It is only just written, but what does that matter?'

He added, 'What is the meaning of the blue flower?'

Karoline saw that he was not going to answer this himself. She said, 'The young man has to go away from his home to find it. He only wants to see it, he does not want to possess it. It cannot be poetry, he knows what that is already. It can't be happiness, he wouldn't need a stranger to tell him what that is, and as far as I can see he is already happy in his home.'

The unlooked-for privilege of the reading was fading and Karoline, still outwardly as calm as she was pale, felt chilled with anxiety. She would rather cut off one of her hands than disappoint him, as he sat looking at her, trusting and intent, with his large light-brown eyes, impatient for a sign of comprehension.

What distressed her most was that after waiting a little, he showed not a hint of resentment or even surprise, but gently shut the notebook. '*Liebe Justen*, it doesn't matter.'

18

The Rockenthiens

In November, the Kreisamtmann took Fritz on a series
of expeditions to local tax offices, whose drowsing inhabitants were brought to reluctant life by their younger
visitor, on fire to learn everything as rapidly as possible.
'The management of an office is not so difficult,' Just
told him. 'It is largely a matter of knowing firstly, what
is coming in, secondly, what is not yet attended to,
thirdly, what has been dealt with and is ready to go out,
and fourthly, what has in fact gone out. Everything must
be at one of these four stages, and there will then be
no excuse of any document being mislaid. For every
transaction there must be a record, and of that record
you must be able to lay your hand immediately on a
written copy. The civilised world could not exist without
its multitude of copying clerks, and they in turn could
not exist if civilisation did not involve so many pieces of
paper.'

'I do not think I could endure life as a copying clerk,'
said Fritz. 'Such occupations should not exist.'

'A revolution would not remove them,' said Coelestin Just, 'you will find that there were copy clerks at the foot of the guillotine.'

As they plodded on together, drops of moisture gathered and slowly fell from their hat-brims, the ends of their noses and the hairy tips of the horses' ears which the animals turned backwards as a kind of protest against the weather. Earth and air were often indistinguishable in the autumn mist, and morning seemed to pass into afternoon without a discernible mid-day. By three o'clock the lamps were already lit in the windows.

It was one of the year's thirteen public holidays, when in Saxony and Thuringia even bread was not baked, but at Greussen Just had asked the local head tax-clerk to keep the office open for an hour or so in the morning. Fritz was explaining how, with the help of chemistry, the copying of documents might perhaps be done automatically. Just sighed.

'Don't suggest any improvements here.'

'The office managers, perhaps, don't welcome our visits,' said Fritz, to whom this idea occurred for the first time, for they were still a strange species to him.

After Greussen, Grüningen, where Just told his young probationary clerk they would take, 'if it is offered', a little refreshment. They turned out of the town up a long drive, bordered with shivering trees and sodden pastures where the autumn grass-burning was still smouldering, sending thin fragrant columns of smoke up to the sky.

'This is the Manor House of Grüningen. We are calling on Herr Kapitän Rockenthien.'

It was a very large house, quite recently built, plastered with yellow stucco.

'Who is the Kapitän Rockenthien?'

'Someone who keeps his doors open,' said the Kreis-amtmann.

Fritz looked ahead and saw that the gate into the coach-yard under the high yellow stone arch, and the great entrance doors on the south side of the house, were in fact standing open. From every tall window the lights shone extravagantly. Perhaps they were expected at Schloss Rockenthien. Fritz never discovered whether that had been so or not.

Two men came out to take their horses, and they went up the three front steps.

'If Rockenthien is at home you will hear him laugh,' said Just, seeming to brace himself up a little, and at that moment, shouting to the servants not to bother, Rockenthien appeared, holding out his broad arms to them, and laughing.

'Coelestin Just, my oldest friend, my best friend.'

'I'm nothing of the sort,' said Just.

'But why did you not bring your niece, the estimable Karoline?'

'I have brought with me this young man, who I am training in business management. Herr Johann Rudolf von Rockenthien, formerly Captain in the army of his Highness Prince Schwarzburg-Sondeshausen, may I present Freiherr Georg Philipp Friedrich von Hardenberg.'

'My youngest friend!' roared von Rockenthien. The good cloth of his jacket strained and creaked as he held out his arms once again. 'You will not be out of place here, I assure you.' His remarks were not quite drowned by the pack of large dogs which had stationed itself in the hall in case something edible was dropped by the goers-in or -out.

'*Platz!*' shouted their master.

Now they were in the *Saal*, which was heated by two great fireplaces, burning spruce and pine. The large number of chairs and tables gave the room the air of a knockdown furniture sale. Who were all these people, all these children? Rockenthien himself scarcely seemed to know, but, as a great joke — like everything else he had said so far — began counting on his fingers. 'My own little ones — Jette, Rudi, Mimi —'

'He will not remember their ages,' called out a peaceful looking blonde woman, not young, lying on a sofa.

'Well, their ages, that is your business, rather than mine. This is my dear wife, Wilhelmine. And here are some, but not all of my stepchildren — George von Kühn, Hans von Kühn, and our Sophie must also be somewhere.'

Fritz looked round about him from one to another, and bowed to the Frau von Rockenthien, who smiled but did not get up, while her husband jovially continued, introducing a French governess, said to have forgotten how to speak the language herself, and a number of callers – our physician, Dr Johann Langermann 'who, unfortunately for himself, can never find anything wrong with us', Herr Regierungsrat Hermann Müller, his wife Frau Regierungsrat Müller, two local attorneys, an instructor from the Luther Gymnasium – all these last, as was clear enough, putting in an hour at the Schloss without any definite invitation. There was, probably, nowhere else much to go in Grüningen.

Young George, who had dashed out of the room as soon as the new visitors were announced, now came back and tugged at the sleeve of Fritz's jacket.

'Heigh-ho, Freiherr von Hardenberg, I've been out to the stable to have a look at your horse. He's no good. Why don't you buy another one?'

Fritz did not heed either George or the company, who like the incoming tide on a shallow beach parted and re-formed behind the interesting newcomer with the object of cutting him off and trying out what he was made of. But he remained fixed, gazing intently down the room.

'His so good manners, where have they gone?' thought Coelestin, who was talking to the Regierungsrat.

At the back of the room, a very young dark-haired girl stood by the window, tapping idly on the glass as though she was trying to attract the attention of someone outside.

'Sophie, why has no-one put up your hair?' called Frau von Rockenthien from her sofa, in an undemanding, indeed soothing tone. 'And why are you looking out of the window?'

'I'm willing it to snow, mother. Then we could all amuse ourselves.'

'Let time stand still until she turns round,' said Fritz, aloud.

'If the soldiers came past, we could throw snow at them,' said Sophie.

'Söphgen, you are twelve years old, and at your age – you don't seem to notice, either, that we have guests,' her mother said.

At this she did turn round, as though caught by a gust, as children do in the wind. 'I'm sorry, I'm sorry.'

19

A Quarter of an Hour

HERR Rockenthien never had quite the air of one to whom the big house at Grüningen – or indeed any house – belonged. At forty, he was large and loose, with impulses as benevolent and ill-directed as a badger-hound's as he trundled through Schloss Grüningen's long corridors.

In point of fact the place had been built fifty years earlier by the father of his wife's first husband, Johann von Kühn. Rockenthien, therefore, had only come into it in 1787, when he married. But he was not the kind of man whose behaviour would be affected by coming into property, or indeed by losing it, and he was not intimidated by finding himself responsible for a large number of other lives.

The district tax office had been established in a relatively small front room to the left of the main entrance. There Rockenthien, in principle, as inheritor of the *Rittergut*, presided, but, though far from a weak man, he was too restless to preside for long over anything.

Coelestin Just, with a clerk, rapidly got through the business.

Fritz told Just: 'Something happened to me.'

Just replied that whatever it was, it must happen later, since his job, indeed his duty, was to come to the front office, where in former days the tenants of Schloss Grüningen had brought in their corn, their firewood and their geese, and now wrestled over their payments in compensation for the field work they no longer did for the Elector of Saxony.

'We have arrived in good time, Hardenberg, but should start at once. It will take us certainly all this morning, then we may expect a good dinner, have no fear of that, then the *Nachtisch*, when we may all talk and express ourselves freely, and the after-dinner sleep, and we may expect to be at work again from four until six.'

'Something has happened to me,' Fritz repeated.

Fritz wrote immediately to Erasmus at the School of Forestry at Hubertusberg, sending the letter by mail coach. Erasmus replied: 'I was at first amazed when I received your letter, but since they have done away with Robespierre in Paris I have become so used to extraordinary happenings that I soon recovered.

'You tell me, that a quarter of an hour decided you. How can you understand a Maiden in a quarter of an hour? If you had said, a quarter of a year, I should have admired your insight into the heart of a woman, but a quarter of an hour, just think of it!

'You are young and fiery, the Maiden is only fourteen and also fiery. You are both sensual human beings and now a tender hour comes and you kiss one another for all you're worth, and when that's over you think, well, this was a Maiden, like other Maidens! But let's suppose you get over all the obstacles, you get married. Then you can indulge as you never could before. But satisfaction makes for weariness, and you end up with what you've always so much dreaded, boredom.'

Fritz was obliged to admit to his brother, from whom he had never had any concealments, that Sophie was not fourteen, but only twelve, and that he hadn't had a tender hour, only the quarter of an hour he had mentioned, surrounded by other people, standing at the great windows of the *Saal* at Schloss Grüningen.

'I am Fritz von Hardenberg,' he had said to her. 'You are Fräulein Sophie von Kühn. You are twelve years of age, I heard your gracious mother say so.'

Sophie put her hands to her hair. 'Up, it should be up.'

'In four years time you will have to consider what man would be fortunate enough to hope to be your husband. Don't tell me that he would have to ask your stepfather! What do you say yourself?'

'In four years time I don't know what I shall be.'

'You mean, you don't know what you will become.'

'I don't want to become.'

'Perhaps you are right.'

'I want to be, and not to have to think about it.'

'But you must not remain a child.'

'I am not a child now.'

'Sophie, I am a poet, but in four years I shall be an administrative official, receiving a salary. That is the time when we shall be married.'

'I don't know you!'

'You have seen me. I am what you see.'

Sophie laughed.

'Do you always laugh at your guests?'

'No, but at Grüningen we don't talk like this.'

'But would you be content to live with me?'

Sophie hesitated, and then said:

'Truly, I like you.'

Erasmus was not reassured. 'Who can guarantee', he wrote, 'that if she is unspoiled now, she will stay unspoiled when she comes out into the world? A commonplace, you will tell me, but commonplaces aren't always wrong. And how can you tell, since you say that she is so beautiful and is sure to be courted by many others, that she won't be untrue to you? Girls act on instinct at thirteen (he still could not quite believe she was any younger), although at twenty-three they are cleverer than we are. Remember what you have said to me so often on this subject – yes, even two months ago, in Weissenfels. Have you forgotten so soon?'

Erasmus went on to say that what had hurt him above all in Fritz's letter was his 'coldly determined manner'. But if he was determined to go ahead, then he could rely on Erasmus for help – his love for his brother was unchanging, its only limit was death. The Father was sure to prove difficult, 'but then we have discussed so often the place of a father in the scheme of things.'

'By the way,' he added, 'what has happened to your friendship with Karoline Just? Fare well! Your true friend and brother, Erasmus.'

20

The Nature of Desire

FRITZ asked whether he might spend Christmas at
Tennstedt. 'That I am quite sure you can, if your own
family will not be disappointed,' said Karoline. 'My uncle
and aunt will make you heartily welcome, and we shall
of course be killing the pig.'

'Justen, something has happened to me.'

He was ill, she had always feared it. 'Tell me what is
wrong.'

'Justen, people might say that we haven't known each
other for long, but your friendship — I cannot tell you
— even when I am away I have such a clear remembrance
of you that I feel as though you are still near me — we
are like two watches set to the same time, and when
we see one another again there has been no interval —
we still strike together.'

She thought: But I could think of nothing to say after
he read me the beginning of his Blue Flower. Thank
God, he doesn't remember that.

'I have fallen in love, Justen.'

'Not at Grüningen!'

She felt as though her body had been hollowed out. Fritz was perplexed. 'Surely you know the family quite well. Herr von Rockenthien welcomed your uncle as his oldest friend.'

'Surely I do know them. But none of the older girls are at home just now, only Söphgen.' She had made this calculation already, when she had heard that her uncle was taking him to Grüningen.

Fritz looked at her steadily.

'Sophie is my heart's heart.'

'But Hardenberg, she can't be much more than . . .' she struggled for moderation. 'And she *laughs*.'

He said, 'Justen, so far you have understood everything, you have listened to everything. But it would be wrong of me to ask too much of you. I see that there is one thing, the most important of all, unfortunately, that you don't grasp, the nature of desire between a man and a woman.'

Karoline could not tell, either then or afterwards, why it was impossible for her to let this pass. Perhaps it was vanity – which was sinful – perhaps the cold fear of losing his confidence for ever.

'Not everyone can speak about what they suffer,' she said. 'Some are separated from the only one they love, but are obliged to remain silent.'

That was not a lie. She had not mentioned herself.

But Fritz's generous sympathy and instant rush of fellow-feeling was very painful to her. What strong force had spoken with her voice and told him something which, after all, *was* a lie and intended as a lie? As the dear Fritz talked on, gently but eagerly, about the obstacles to happiness (he would of course ask her nothing more, what she had told him was sacred) – the obstacles which drew them even more closely together – she saw that between them they had created out of nothing a new and most unwelcome entity. So that now there were four of them, the poet, the much-desired Sophie screaming with laughter, herself, the sober niece-housekeeper, and now her absent, secret, frustrated lover, doubtless a respectable minor official of more than thirty, probably – as Karoline increasingly clearly saw him – in sober clothes of hard-wearing material, almost certainly a married man, or he might, perhaps, be a pastor. He was so real at that moment that she could have put out a hand and touched him. And he had been born entirely from the wound that Hardenberg had dealt her, when he told her that she did not understand the nature of desire.

'Words are given us to understand each other, even if not completely,' Fritz went on in great excitement.

'And to write poetry.'

'Yes that's so, Justen, but you mustn't ask too much of language. Language refers only to itself, it is not the key to anything higher. Language speaks, because speaking is its pleasure and it can do nothing else.'

'In that case it might as well be nonsense,' objected Karoline.

'Why not? Nonsense is only another language.'

21

Snow

BUT Fritz, after all, was obliged to spend Christmas at Weissenfels. Sidonie wrote to him that not only would the Bernhard be much disappointed if he did not come, but that he must see his new brother. In the warmth of the great curtained patriarchal goose-featherbed at Weissenfels Nature's provisions continued, so that last year Amelie had been conceived and born, and this year, Christoph. The Bernhard had received the news without enthusiasm. 'There are now two more younger than myself, it will be hard for me to attract sufficient attention.'

'But you love little Christoph,' said Sidonie patiently. 'You are only a child yourself, Bernhard, you are still in your days of grace.'

'On the whole, I hate little Christoph. When does Fritz come? Will he be here for Christmas Eve?'

At Tennstedt, Karoline and Rahel together saw to the cabbages buried in sand in the cellar, and the potatoes buried in earth in the yard. The surplus provisions were arranged in a deep cupboard just inside the kitchen for distribution to the poor, together with double rations of schnaps which harboured in every coarse, consoling mouthful the memory of the heat of summer.

About Hardenberg they only remarked to each other that it was a pity, after all, that he could not spend Christmas with them.

On his way to Weissenfels, Fritz was somewhat delayed. He had arranged to call in for a few hours at Schloss Grüningen. But that evening, all over the administrative district of Thuringia and Saxony, it began to snow. The north-east wind outlined every twig, every cart-shaft, every cabbage-stump, with a rim of crystalline white. Then that disappeared and there was nothing but a white blindness that seemed at the same time to be rising from the ground and falling from the heavy sky.

While Karoline was helping to clear a path to the outside pump, a letter arrived from Hardenberg, from Grüningen. 'So he has got no further!' In it he told her, perhaps not very tactfully, that being marooned, he was sleeping and eating 'in the most hospitable house in the world'. The snow was so deep, he alleged, that he couldn't go out without danger, and to take pointless risks was unworthy of a responsible man. 'I shall, I will, I must, I ought, I can stay here, who can do anything against Fate? I have decided that I am a Determinist. Fate might not be so kind another time.'

'In that great house there must be someone who can clear the carriageway,' Karoline told herself. 'But he has always talked a great deal of nonsense. When he first came here, he said my hands were beautiful, also the tablecloth and the tea-tray.'

He had enclosed some verses, which ended,

Allow me a glimpse of the future, when our hearts
Are no longer full of anxiety and resignation, and Love
*   and Fortune*
Reward us at last for our sacrifices, and far behind us
Roars youth's wild ocean.
Some day, in the noon-tide of life, we shall both sit at
*   table,*
Each of us will be married, with the one we love
*   beside us,*
Then we shall look back to how it was in the
*   morning.*
Who would have dreamed of this? Never does the
*   heart sigh in vain!*

Karoline knew that 'Never does the heart sigh in vain!' was the sort of thing that they printed on sweet papers. But the last verse caused her anguish. There he was, her non-existent admirer, the unloved *Verliebte*, conjured out of her own unhappiness, sitting at table with her, indeed, all four of them were there. But the poem, at least, was for her and her alone. The title was 'Reply to Karoline'.

She put it in the drawer where she kept such things, and turned the key. Then she clasped her arms round her body as if to ward off the cold.

22

Now Let Me Get To Know Her

DURING his two days with the Rockenthiens, Fritz marvelled at the difference between daily life in the Kloster Gasse at Weissenfels and at Schloss Grüningen. At Grüningen there were no interrogations, no prayer-meetings, no anxiety, no catechisms, no fear. Anger, if any, evaporated within a few moments, and there was a good deal of what, at Weissenfels, would be called time-wasting. At breakfast time, no-one at Grüningen slammed down their coffee-cups, and cried out '*Satt!*' The constant coming and going round the tranquil Frau Rockenthien (who, like the Freifrau von Hardenberg, had a new baby to nurse) seemed an image of perpetual return, so that time scarcely declared itself an enemy.

At Grüningen, mention of the goings-on of the French caused no distress. When George appeared in a tricolour waistcoat there was not even a murmur of surprise. With pain Fritz compared the Demon George, easy-going and noisy, with the strangeness of the Bernhard. Then again, Uncle Wilhelm's visits at Weissenfels were an occasion of dread, one prayed for him to leave, while at Grüningen relations and friends poured in indiscriminately, all of them greeted, even if they had been there only yesterday, as if they had not been seen for many months.

'When summer comes we have the *Nachtisch* outside, under the lilacs,' Frau Rockenthien told him. 'Then you must read aloud to us.' At Weissenfels, after meals, everyone dispersed as soon as grace was said. Fritz was not sure whether there were any lilacs in the garden or not. He was inclined to think not.

Snowed-up for probably not more than a day or two, Fritz knew he must use his time wisely. 'You have your wish now, Fräulein Sophie,' he said, watching her stand by the same window in the *Saal*. Her child's pink mouth was just open, as without knowing it she put out her tongue a very little, longing to taste the crystal flakes on the far side of the glass. Herr Rockenthien, thundering past with George and Hans at his heels, paused to ask Fritz about his studies. He asked everyone he met, with genuine interest, about their occupations, a habit he had picked up during his service with the Prince of Schwarzburg-Sondeshausen as a commissioning officer. Fritz talked eagerly about chemistry, geology and philosophy. He mentioned Fichte. 'Fichte explained to us that there is only one absolute self, one identity for all humanity.'

'Well, this Fichte is lucky,' cried Rockenthien. 'In this household I have thirty-two identities to consider.'

'Papa hasn't a care in the world,' said George. 'Today, when he was desperately needed by the head gardener to give instructions about the blocked ditches, he was out shooting in the snow.'

'My career has been in the army, not in the vegetable patch,' said Rockenthien good-humouredly. 'As to shooting, it is not a passion with me. I was out with my gun early this morning in order to feed my family.' With the air of a conjuror, he drew out of his pocket what he had evidently forgotten until now, a string of small dead birds connected head to tail with a length of thread. It seemed as though the procession – one or two of them stuck, and he had to tug and heave – would go on forever.

'Linnets! They won't go far!' shouted George. 'Three at a time I could crunch them.'

'All feel that I have nothing to do,' said Herr Rocken- thien, 'although in truth this is one of our busiest times, and it will be one of my responsibilities to see that order is kept during the Advent Fair.'

'Where is this fair?' asked Fritz – it's not in order to *fichtisieren* here, he told himself – better to say no more about it.

'Oh, at Greussen, two miles away,' cried Sophie. 'It is the only thing that ever happens here, except the sum- mer and the autumn fairs, and they also are at Greussen.'

'But you haven't yet been to the Leipzig fair?' Fritz asked her.

No, Sophie had never even so much as been to Leipzig. At the very thought of it her eyes shone, her lips parted.

What or whom does she look like? he thought, with this rich hair, and her long, pretty nose, not at all like her mother's. Nor were her arched eyebrows. In the third volume of Lavater's *Physiognomische Fragmente* there was an illustration, after a copperplate by Johann Heinrich Lips, of Raphael's self-portrait at the age of twenty-five. This picture had exactly the air of Sophie. From the copperplate, of course, you couldn't tell the colour, or the tonality of the flesh, only that the expression was unworldly and humane and that the large eyes were dark as night.

In his first quarter of an hour, at the window of the great *Saal*, Fritz had already opened his heart to Sophie. Now let me get to know her, he thought. How difficult will that be?

'If we are going to spend our lives together,' he said, 'I should like to learn everything about you.'

'Yes, but you must not call me *du*.'

'Very well, I will not, until you give me permission.'

He thought, let's make the attempt, even though it's possible that she would rather play with the little brother and sister. They were on the long, broad terrace between the house and the garden, which had been swept almost clear of snow. Mimi and Rudi, young and obstreperous, ran beside them with their iron-bound hoops. '*Lass das*, Freiherr, you don't know how to hit it,' Rudi had cried sharply, but Fritz did know, having been brought up in a house of many hoops, and he whacked first one and then the other hard and true so that they spun away and had to be pursued almost out of sight.

'Now, tell me what you think about poetry.'

'I don't think about it at all,' said Sophie.

'But you would not want to hurt a poet's feelings.'

'I would not want to hurt anyone's feelings.'

'Let us speak of something else. What do you like best to eat?'

Cabbage soup, Sophie told him, and a nice smoked eel.

'What is your opinion of wine and tobacco?'

'Those, too, I like.'

'Do you smoke, then?'

'Yes, my stepfather gave me a pipe.'

'And music?'

'Ah, that I love. A few months ago there were some students in the town and they played a serenade.'

'What did they play?'

'They played "Wenn die Liebe in deinen blauen Augen". That of course could not be for me, my eyes are dark, but it was very beautiful.'

Singing, yes. Dancing, yes, most certainly, but she was

not permitted to attend the public balls until she was fourteen.

'Do you remember the question I asked you when I first met you, by the window?'

'No, I don't remember it.'

'I asked you whether you had thought at all about marriage.'

'Oh, I am afraid of that.'

'You did not say that when we spoke of it by the window.'

She repeated, 'I am afraid of that.' After Rudi, with Mimi whimpering after him, had returned and been dismissed again ('Poor souls! They are getting out of breath!' said Sophie.) he asked her about her faith. She answered readily. They kept the days of penitence, of course, and on Sundays they went to the church, but she did not believe everything that was said there. She did not believe in life after death.

'But Sophie, Jesus Christ returned to earth!'

'That was all very well for him,' said Sophie. 'I respect the Christus, but if I was to walk and talk again after I was dead, that would be ridiculous.'

'What does your stepfather say when you tell him you don't believe?'

'He laughs.'

'But when you were younger, what did your teacher tell you? Surely you must have had a teacher?'

'Yes, until I was eleven.'

'Who was he?'

'The Magister Kegel from the seminary here in Grüningen.'

'Did you pay him attention?'

'Once he was angry with me.'

'Why?'

'He could not believe that I could understand so little.'

'What could you not understand?'

'Figures, and numbers.'

'Numbers are not more difficult to understand than music.'

'Ach, well, Kegel beat me.'

'Surely not, Sophie.'

'Yes, he struck me.'

'But what did your stepfather say to that?'

'Ach, well, it was difficult for him. A teacher must be obeyed.'

'What did the Magister Kegel do?'

'He collected the money that was owing to him, and left the house.'

'But what did he say?'

' "*On reviendra, mam'zell.*" '

'But he did not come back?'

'No, now I am too old to learn anything.'

She looked at him a little anxiously and added, 'Perhaps if I saw a miracle, as they did in the old days, I should believe more.'

'Miracles don't make people believe!' Fritz cried. 'It's the belief that is the miracle.'

He saw that, having done her best, she looked disappointed, and went on: 'Sophie, listen to me. I am going to tell you what I felt, when I first saw you standing by the window. When we catch sight of certain human figures and faces . . . especially certain eyes, expressions, movements — when we hear certain words, when we read certain passages, thoughts take on the meaning of laws . . . a view of life true to itself, without any self-estrangement. And the self is set free, for the moment, from the constant pressure of change . . . Do you understand me?'

Sophie nodded. 'Yes, I do. I have heard of that before. Some people are born again and again into this world.'

Fritz persevered. 'I did not quite mean that. But Schlegel, too, is interested in transmigration. Should you like to be born again?'

Sophie considered a little. 'Yes, if I could have fair hair.'

Herr von Rockenthien pressed young Hardenberg to stay longer. If he noticed that this son of an ancient house was courting his stepdaughter, he was not at all against it, although it might be said that his temperament led him to encourage almost everything. Frau von Rockenthien, serene and apparently in radiant health, but supported by cushions numberless, also nodded kindly. She mentioned, however, that Sophie's elder sister, Friederike von Mandelsloh, would soon be coming back home to Grüningen on a long visit, and would be a companion for Söphgen.

'Let them all come back to us, I say,' Rockenthien declared. 'Partings are painful! Isn't that what they sing at Jena at the end of the year, when the students leave?'

'They do,' said Fritz, and Rockenthien, in a voice as deep as the third level of a copper-mine, but with inappropriate cheerfulness, broke into the plaintive song: '*Scheiden und meiden tut weh . . .*'

'Now that I am leaving your hospitable roof, I should like your permission to write a letter to your stepdaughter Sophie,' said Fritz. Rockenthien broke off his song, and gathering the tattered remnants of his responsibilities around him, said that there would be no objection, as long as her mother opened it and read through it first.

'Of course. And I should like her, if you see fit, to be permitted to write an answer.'

'Permission! If that is all that is needed, I permit!'

23

I Can't Comprehend Her

FRITZ wrote in his journal, 'I can't comprehend her, I can't get the measure of her. I love something that I do not understand. She has got me, but she is not at all sure she wants me. Her stepfather is an influence upon her, and I see now that jollity is as relentless as piety. Indeed she has told me that she would always like to see me cheerful. He also, of course, gave her a tobacco pipe.

'August Schlegel wrote that "form is mechanical when, through external force, it is imparted merely as an accidental addition without reference to its quality: as, for example, when we give a particular shape to a soft mass so that it may retain the same when it hardens. Organic form is innate: it unfolds itself from within, and acquires its determination at the same time as the perfect development of the germ."

'That, surely, is what is happening with Sophie. I do not want to change her, but I admit that I should like to feel that I could do so if necessary. But, in twelve years, during which she did not know that I existed on this earth, she has "acquired her determination". I should be happier if I could see one opening, the shadow of an opening, where I could make myself felt a little.

'To decide that she does not believe in the life to come. What insolence, what enormity.

'She said, "Truly, I like you."

'She wants to please everyone, but will not adapt herself. Her face, her body, her enjoyment of life, her health, that which she likes to speak of. Her little dogs. Has her temperament woken up yet? Her fear of ghosts, her wine-drinking. Her hand on her cheek.'

At the house in the Kloster Gasse his mother was still lying in after the birth of Christoph, who was thriving only moderately, in spite of a capacious wet-nurse brought in from one of the villages. Uncomplaining as always on her own account, she was distressed now only for her infant, and for the Bernhard. Someone might be disillusioning him − (she feared this every Christmas) − and, without intending to do so, destroy his belief in Knecht Rupert.

'I don't remember the Bernhard ever believing in Knecht Rupert,' said Fritz to Sidonie. 'He always knew it was old Dumpfin, from the bakery, in a false beard.'

He had confided his secret only to Karoline Just, to Erasmus, and to Sidonie, who agreed that it would not do at the moment, or indeed at any moment, to agitate their mother. Fritz dragged Sidonie to his own room, where he took down the third volume from his own set of Lavater's *Physiognomie*. 'That is my Söphgen to the life. It is Raphael's self-portrait, of course . . . But how can a girl of twelve look like a genius of twenty-five?'

'That is easy,' said Sidonie. 'She cannot.'

'But you have never so much as seen her.'

'That's true. But I *shall* see her, I suppose, and when I do I shall tell you exactly the same thing.'

He shut the book. 'My pockets are full of things I've bought.' He took out handfuls of gingerbread, needle-cases, eau de Cologne, a bird-charmer and a catapult. 'Where can I put them, Sidonie? You don't know how uncomfortable they are. Torment!'

'In the library, that's where I'm going to have the gift-giving.' Sidonie, while attentive to the timid and plaintive requests occasionally brought to her from her mother's room, was entirely in charge. She had already made the stable-boys bring fir-tree boughs into the house and heap them up in the library. She kept the key herself. Whenever she opened the door an overwhelmingly spicy green breath crowded out into the passage, as though the forest had marched into the house.

'I bought all these on the way, at Freyburg,' Fritz said. 'I suppose you've been getting up every morning before it's light, as you always did, making things.'

'I hate sewing,' said Sidonie, 'and I am not good at it, and never shall be, but yes, I have.'

Where was Erasmus? Karl had arrived, Anton was there, the Freiherr had been obliged to go over to the salt mines at Artern, but would be back on Christmas Eve. 'That is what is so strange, Fritz, Asmus set off to ride to Grüningen to meet you.'

'Ride! What is he riding?'

'Oh, Karl's orderly brought a second horse with him, from the remount section.'

'That's fortunate.'

'Not so fortunate for Asmus, because he can't manage this horse, he has already fallen off twice.'

'Someone will pick him up, the roads are crowded now that the snow is clearing. But why is he going to Grüningen? *Weiss Gott*, it's idiotic!'

Sidonie arranged and rearranged the pile of bright things which Fritz had brought with him.

'I think he wanted to see for himself what your Sophie looked like.'

24

The Brothers

'Fritz!'

Erasmus caught up with his brother on the front door steps, racing after him up the right-hand flight, dislodging Lukas, the houseman, and his broom.

'Fritz, I have seen her, yes, I've been to Grüningen! I talked to your Sophie and to a friend of hers, and to the family.'

Fritz stood as if turned to ice, and Erasmus called out, 'Best of brothers, she won't do!'

He threw his arms round his so much taller brother. 'She won't do at all, my Fritz. She is good-natured, yes, but she is not your intellectual equal. Great Fritz, you are a philosopher, you are a poet.'

Lukas disappeared with his broom, hastening to the kitchen door to repeat what he had heard.

'Who gave you permission to present yourself at Grüningen?' asked Fritz, so far almost calm.

'Fritz, Sophie is stupid!'

'Mad, Erasmus!'

'No, I'm not mad, best of all Fritzes!'

'I said, who gave you permission—'

'Her mind is empty—'

'Better silence—!'

'Empty as a new jug, Fritz—'

'Silence!'

Erasmus clung on. And there, on the front steps of the house in the Kloster Gasse, the two of them were on show, and once again the people of Weissenfels, as they went by at a foot's pace, were scandalised, as they had been by the Bernhard's escapade on the banks of the river. There were the eldest of the Hardenberg boys, the Freiherr's pride, almost at blows.

Erasmus was by far the more upset of the two. His breath steamed up like a kettle in the winter's air. Without effort Fritz, trying for calm, pinned him against the iron handrail. 'You mean well, *Junge*, I am sure you do. Your feelings are those of a brother. You think I have been taken in by a beautiful face.'

'No, I don't,' Erasmus protested. 'You are taken in, yes, but not by a beautiful face. Fritz, she is not beautiful, she is not even pretty. I say again this Sophie is empty-headed, moreover at twelve years old she has a double chin—'

'Gracious Freiin, your brothers are knocking each other's teeth out on the front steps,' announced Lukas. 'Peace and fellowship have been forgotten, indeed they are now at full length in the Kloster Gasse.'

'I will go to them at once,' said Sidonie.

'Shall I inform the Freifrau?'

'Don't be a fool, Lukas.'

Erasmus had been warmly received on his entirely unannounced visit to Grüningen. He was welcome for his brother's sake, and Frau Rockenthien had a special tenderness for small and insignificant young people, believing that they could be transformed, by giving them plenty to eat, into tall and stout ones. But Sophie herself, to his horror, he found was no more than a very noisy, very young girl, not at all like his own sisters. During the scant two hours of his visit she and a friend of hers, a Jette Goldacker, had invited him to walk with them down to the path by the River Helbe, since they must not go alone, and see the Hussars, who were quite drunk, and were toppling over on the ice, the Regimental Sergeant too, and everything was going flying pitsch! patsch! It was Jette, true, who had drawn attention to a corporal unbuttoning himself, but Sophie had not reproached her. For *morgen*, Sophie said *morchen*, for *spät* she said *späd*, for Hardenberg, 'Hardenburch'. Well, Erasmus did not care a snap how she spoke. He did not set himself up as a teacher of elocution. But never had he met a young maiden of good family with so little restraint.

Fritz must have lost his senses. 'You're intoxicated. It's a *Rausch*, think of yourself as *im Rausch*. It will wear off, in the course of nature it must.'

Because of the Christmas gathering and because the Freiherr might come back at any moment, no more could be said between them, and after all the quarrel arose not from enmity but from love, although that was not likely to make it easier to settle. A truce was called.

'I know that I am receiving moral grace. How can that be intoxication?' Fritz wrote.

> *Am I to be kept apart from her for ever?*
> *Is the hope of being united*
> *With what we recognised as our own*
> *But could not quite possess completely*
> *Is that too to be called intoxication?*
> *All humanity will be, in time, what Sophie*
> *Is now for me: human perfection — moral grace —*
> *Life's highest meaning will then no longer*
> *Be mistaken for drunken dreams.*

25

Christmas at Weissenfels

'WHAT are the boys saying?' asked the Freifrau doubtfully. She had been permitted to move out of the large shabby marital bedroom and upstairs, with the baby, to somewhere much smaller, almost an attic, which was sometimes used for storing apples, so that, in spite of the cold, it never lost its lazy, bittersweet apple smell. Only the wet nurse and a lady's maid who had come with her from her old home when she married, creaked up the stairs as far as this — Sidonie, too, of course, on flying feet.

'Ah, Sidonie, my dear, I thought I heard their voices raised, though not so much to-day as yesterday . . . Tell me, what is Fritz talking about?'

'About moral grace, mother.'

At this watchword of the Herrnhut the Freifrau sank back in relief against the starched pillows.

'And you have got the library ready — you know your father likes to —'

'Of course, of course,' said Sidonie.

'Tell me whether you think little Christoph is any better.'

Sidonie, an expert, removed several layers of shawls and looked closely at her frail brother. He scowled at her manfully, she brightened. 'Yes, truly, he is much better.'

'Thank God, thank God, I should not say this, she is another Christian soul, but I do not at all like the wet nurse.'

'I will speak to her at once,' said Sidonie, 'and send her back to Elsterdorf.'

'And then —?' Sidonie thought her mother was worrying about a replacement, but saw it was not so. 'You are thinking about moving back to your bedroom downstairs. No, you are not well enough yet for that. I will send for your coffee.'

The Freiherr followed the old custom, which most of Weissenfels' households had given up, of the Christmas reckoning. The mother spoke to her daughters, the father to his sons, and told them first what had displeased, then what had pleased most in their conduct during the past year. In addition, the young Hardenbergs were asked to make a clean breast of anything that they should have told their parents, but had not. The Freifrau would not be well enough to undertake this duty, and the Freiherr, it was thought, might arrive from Artern later than he had calculated. But he arrived precisely at the time he had said.

Christmas Eve was bright and windless. All day the knocker of the kitchen door echoed through the yards. No-one who asked for charity at the Hardenbergs' house was ever turned away empty-handed, but on this day they could expect something more substantial. At Ober-wiederstadt the pressure had been much greater. The house had been very near the border, and many who had no permission to cross into Prussia, and indeed were not particularly welcome in any of the states — the vagrants, old soldiers, travelling theatrical companies, ped-lars — all these silted up on the frontier like floating rubbish on a river's banks. In Weissenfels there were only the town poor and the town mad, and later the girls with unwanted pregnancies, who could not afford the services of the Angel-maker, the back-street abortionist. These girls did not come to the kitchen door until it was quite dark.

In the library candles had been attached, waiting to blaze, on every sprig of the heaped-up fir branches. The tables were laid with white cloths, a table for each soul in the household. On each table was placed a name, made out of almond paste and baked brown. The presents themselves were not labelled. One must guess, or perhaps never know, who were the givers.

'What are we expected to sing for Christmas Eve?' Karl asked.

'I don't know,' said Sidonie. 'Father likes Reichardt's "Welcome to this Vale of Sorrow."'

'Bernhard,' said Karl, 'you are not to eat the almond-paste letters.'

The Bernhard was wounded. It had been almost two years now since he cared anything about sweets.

'I dare say too that this is the last year I shall be called upon to sing a treble solo,' he said. 'Pubescence is at the door.'

'What I want to know is this,' cried Erasmus, 'I want to know from you, our Fritz, what you will say when Father asks us to confess what we have done during the year. You know what I have already written to you, that you can rely upon me in everything. But are you going to tell him, as you have told me, not that you are in love, that needs no more apology than a bird needs an apology to fly, no, but that you have committed yourself to a little girl of twelve who laughs through her fingers to see a drunk in the snow?'

'Of this you have told me nothing,' said Karl reproachfully. Bernhard, although attached to Fritz, was in ecstasies, foreseeing embarrassments of all kinds.

'I shall tell him nothing that is unworthy of Sophie,' Fritz declared. 'Her name means wisdom. She is my wisdom, she is my truth.'

'Freiin, the lights,' said Lukas, hurrying in. 'Your gracious father is coming down to the library.'

'Well, help me, then, Lukas.' He had left the door open and they saw the household assembled outside, their aprons patches of white in the shadows of the hall. At Grüningen they would have been in uproar on a holiday like this, but not in the Kloster Gasse.

Inside the library the myriad fiery shining points of light threw vast shadows of the fir branches onto the high walls and even across the ceiling. In the warmth the room breathed even more deeply, more resinously, more greenly. On the tables the light sparkled across gold-painted walnuts, birds in cages, dormice in their nests, dolls made of white bread twisted into shape, hymnbooks, Fritz's needle-cases and little bottles of *Kölnischwasser*, Sidonie's embroidery, oddments made out of willow and birch, pocket-knives, scissors, pipes, wooden spoons with curious handles which made them almost unusable, religious prints mounted on brilliant sheets of tin. By contrast with this sparkle and display how worn, as he came in, how haggard in spite of its roundness, was the face of the Freiherr von Hardenberg. As he paused at the door to give some instructions to Lukas, Fritz said to Karl, 'He is old, but I cannot bring myself to make things easy for him.'

The Freiherr came in, and quite against precedent, sat down in the elbow chair. His family looked at him in dismay. It had been his habit on Christmas Eve to stand behind the large leather-covered desk, always kept clear of presents and candles, in the very centre of the library.

'Why does he do this?' muttered Erasmus.

'I don't know,' said Fritz. 'Schlegel tells me that Goethe has bought one of these chairs, but when he sits in it he can't think.'

As their father began to speak he beat his hand, as though marking time, on the embracing arm of the chair.

'You expect me to consider your conduct for the past year, both the progress you have made and your backsliding. You expect me to question you about anything that has been concealed from me. You expect — indeed it would be your duty — to answer me truthfully. You expect these things, but you are mistaken. On this Christmas Eve, the Christmas Eve of the year 1794, I shall want no confessions, I shall make no interrogations. What is the reason for this? Well, in reality, while at Artern I received a letter from a very old friend, the Former Prediger of the Brethren at Neudietendorf. It was a Christmas letter, reminding me that I was fifty-six years of age and could not, in the nature of things, expect more than another few years on this earth. The Prediger instructed me for once not to reprove, but to remember only that this is a day of unspeakable joy, on which all men and women should be no more, and no less, than children. And therefore,' he added, looking slowly round at the sparkling tables, the wooden spoons, the golden nuts, 'I myself have become, during this sacred time, wholly a child.'

Anything less childlike than the leathery, seamed, broad, bald face of the Freiherr and his eyes, perplexed to the point of anguish under his strong eyebrows, could hardly be imagined. Probably the Prediger had not tried to imagine it. The Brethren were experienced in joy, and perhaps sometimes forgot what a difficult emotion it is, and how unfamiliar to many. Heavily the Freiherr von Hardenberg looked up from the desk.

'Are we not to have music?'

The Bernhard, disappointed at his father's strange mildness, but pleased to see his elders disconcerted, shinned up the library steps used for the highest shelves, and began to sing, in what was still a child's voice of absolute purity, 'He is born, let us love him.' The angelic voice was taken as a signal for the patiently-waiting household to come in, bringing with them the two-year-old Amelie, who advanced with determination on anything that shone, and a bundle of wrappings, which was the infant Christoph. The candle-flames began to burn low and catch the evergreens, there was a snapping and hissing and trails of sweet smoke as they were calmly extinguished by Sidonie. The room was still, in alternate patches, brilliant and shadowy as everyone went to search for their own tables.

Erasmus stood close to Fritz. 'What will you tell Father now?'

26

The Mandelsloh

NOTHING. Fritz would accept what Fate and Chance sent
and take the opportunity to say nothing. The distance
between himself and Erasmus distressed him far more
than any falling-out with his father.

At Neudietendorf he had learned, even when he
thought he was refusing to learn, the Moravian respect
for chance. Chance is one of the manifestations of God's
will. If he had stayed on among the Brethren, even his
wife would have been chosen for him by lot. Chance had
brought the Prediger's letter to Artern quicker than
could have been expected, and made it possible for him
to delay discussing his marriage to Sophie until somewhat
nearer the time when he might expect to earn his own
living. But chance, as he knew, might at any moment
restore his father to his usual state of furious impatience.
He had only spoken of being joyous, after all, for one
day.

On Silvesterabend, six days after Christmas, Fritz
received a letter from Sophie.

Dear Hardenberg,

In the first place I thank you for your letter secondly for your hair and thirdly for the sweet Needle-case which has given me much pleasure. You ask me whether you may be allowed to write to me? You can be assured that it is pleasant to me at All Times to read a letter from you. You know dear Hardenberg I must write no more.

Sophie von Kühn

'She is my wisdom,' said Fritz.

Back on a day's visit to Grüningen, in the New Year of 1795, Fritz asked the Hausherr Rockenthien, 'Why must she write no more? Am I then dangerous?'

'My dear Hardenberg, she must write no more because she scarcely knows how to. Send for her schoolmaster and enquire of him! Certainly she ought to have studied more, ha! ha! Then she could well have written correctly a sweetheart's letter.'

'I don't want correctness, but I should like them a good deal longer,' said Fritz.

His next letter from Sophie ran: 'You gave me some of your Hair and I wrapped it nicely in a little Bit of paper and put it in the drawer of a table. The other day when I wanted to take it out neither the Hair nor the Bit of paper was to be seen. Now please have your Hair cut again, and in particular the Hair of your head.'

The next time he was at Grüningen, a strong blonde young woman came into the room, carrying a bucket. 'God help me, but I've forgotten what I meant to do with this,' she said, slamming it down on the painted wooden floor.

'This is my elder sister Friederike,' said Sophie eagerly. 'She is the Frau Leutnant Mandelsloh.'

She is not like her mother, Fritz thought, and not at all like her sister.

'Frieke, he wants me to write him another letter.'

Fritz said, 'No, Frau Leutnant, I want her to write me many hundreds of letters.'

'Well, the attempt shall be made,' said the Mandelsloh. 'But she will need some ink.'

'Is there none in the house?' Fritz asked. 'It is the same with us, we are often short of soap, or some other commodity.'

'Here there is plenty of everything,' said the Mandelsloh. 'And there is ink in my stepfather's study, and in several other rooms. Everywhere we may take what we like. But Söphgen does not use ink every day.'

Sophie was gone. Left alone with this large-boned, fair-haired creature, Fritz followed his instinct, turning to her at once for advice. 'Frau Leutnant, would you recommend me to ask your stepfather whether he would consent to an engagement between myself and –'

'About that I can't advise you at all,' she said calmly.

'You must see how much courage you have. The difficulty is not what to ask people, but when. I suppose your father, too, must be taken into account.'

'That is so,' said Fritz.

'Well, perhaps the two of them will sit down comfortably together and enjoy a good pipe of tobacco.' Fritz tried, but failed, to imagine this. 'In that way everything may be settled without tears. My own husband was an orphan. There was no-one he had to consider when he came to discuss matters with my stepfather, except his unmarried sister, whom of course he must support.'

'I thank you for your advice,' said Fritz. 'I think, indeed, that women have a better grasp on the whole business of life than we men have. We are morally better than they are, but they can reach perfection, we can't. And that is in spite of the fact that they particularise, we generalise.'

'That I have heard before. What is wrong with particulars? Someone has to look after them.'

Fritz paced the room. Conversation had the same effect on him as music.

'Furthermore, I believe that all women have what Schlegel finds lacking in so many men, a beautiful soul. But so often it is concealed.'

'Very likely it is,' said the Mandelsloh. 'What do you think of mine?'

Having said this, she looked startled, as though someone else had spoken. Fritz, who had reached the point nearest to her and to her bucket, stopped and fixed on her his brilliant, half-wild gaze.

'Don't look so interested!' she cried. 'I am very dull. My husband is very dull. We are two dull people. I should not have mentioned us. Even to think of us might make you weep from boredom.'

'But I don't find −'

She put her hands over her ears.

'No, don't say it! We who are dull accept that intelligent persons should run the world and the rest of us should work six days a week to keep them going, if only it turns out that they know what they are doing.'

'We are not talking about myself,' cried Fritz. 'We are talking about your soul, Frau Leutnant.'

Sophie reappeared, without pen, paper or ink. It seemed that she had been playing with some new kittens in the housemaids' pantry. 'So that is where they are,' said the Mandelsloh. She was reminded now that she had brought the bucket of water to drown these kittens. The servants were faint-hearted about their duty in this respect.

Friederike von Mandelsloh had been living in the garrison town of Langensalza, with her husband, a leutnant in Prince Clemens' Regiment. She had come back home to Grüningen, about ten miles away, because he had been sent to France with the Rheinfeld expeditionary force. She lamented that she had never been able to live long enough anywhere to have a carpet laid properly (and she did possess a large Turkish carpet). But then, she was a soldier's wife. Although she was, of course, no real relation to Hausherr Rockenthien she was, of all the younger generation, his favourite. In spite of her brusque semi-military manner, developed since she married at the age of sixteen, her china-blue eyes suggested her mother's assurance, her mother's calm. 'You are the best of the lot,' he told Friederike. 'You should never have left the house. It amounted to cruelty to myself.'

Every man, Rockenthien thought, deserved such a presence in his house. The Mandelsloh would check over the wines in the cellar, do his accounts, drown the kittens, keep an eye, if necessary, on Söphgen. And Friederike did take charge, not (as Sidonie did at Weissenfels) out of pity and painful anxiety, but simply as the result of her mother's smiling ability to impose on her. Frau Rockenthien's only positive action since Günther was born and Hardenberg had attached himself to Sophie had been to get Friederike back into the house. Beyond that, however, nothing was really necessary.

27

Erasmus Calls on Karoline Just

KAROLINE Just had never met Erasmus, but even at the door, before the servant announced him she knew who he must be. He was short and slight, his face was round, his eyes were neither large nor bright, but he was Fritz's brother. She also knew from what she had been told about him that he must be due back, overdue perhaps, for his next term at Hubertusberg.

Coelestin and Rahel Just were out. They were very much occupied at the moment with the purchase of a garden plot within walking distance of their street. They would grow asparagus, yes, and melons, and build a garden house, an earthly Paradise. They had gone out to drink coffee with the neighbours and to discuss the project, about which everybody already knew everything. Karoline, of course, was invited. But she did not go out very much these days.

'I am afraid there is no-one but myself to welcome you,' she said. 'Your brother of course is still lodging with us, but he is on a visit to Grüningen.'

Erasmus had come on a wave of tenderness and an impulse of conscience towards Karoline, or rather towards Karoline as he imagined her, which should properly have been felt by Fritz. He needed, too, to share his dismay at the intrusion into his life of such a creature as Sophie with someone who would surely understand him. He hoped at the same time to find out rather more about her, since his dispute with his brother meant that they could no longer discuss the matter, even in a letter.

'Fräulein, I speak to you in all sincerity.'

She asked him to call her Karoline.

'You must know Schloss Grüningen quite well, isn't that so? Your Uncle Just goes there, and must sometimes have taken you with him.'

'Yes, he has,' said Karoline. 'What do you want to know about it?' But Erasmus broke out, 'What do you think of her? Who is she, truly?'

'I was naturally more the friend of her eldest sister, who has married now and left home.'

'Speak to me honestly, Karoline.'

She asked him, 'Have you never met Sophie von Kühn?'

'I have. I went to Schloss Grüningen and knocked at the door, as I have knocked at yours. I no longer have any decent manners, or any explanation for my conduct. Perhaps I am going mad.'

'So, you have seen her. She is mature for her age, in

some ways. She walks gracefully. She has pretty hair, dark hair, that is a good point.' For the first time she looked frankly at Erasmus. 'How could he?'

'I hoped that you would answer that. I came here in the hope that you might tell me that, and also because —'

Karoline collected herself enough to pull the bell. 'I am going to ask them to bring some refreshments, which we don't want.'

'Of course we do not,' said Erasmus, who, however, when it arrived, ate large quantities of *Zwieback*, and drank some wine.

He is twenty years only, she thought. He pities me. Never again will he have such sympathy for another human being whom he does not even know. But she did not want to be pitied. 'Wait here a minute.' She left him sitting there, uncertain what to do — he did not like to go on eating while she was out of the room — and came back with the verses which Hardenberg had sent her:

Some day, in the noon-tide of life, we shall both sit at table,
Each of us will be married, with the one we love beside us,
Then we shall look back to how it was in the morning —
Who would have dreamed of this? Never does the heart sigh in
   vain!

Erasmus sat there, almost beyond words humiliated and embarrassed. 'Four of you then, Karoline, I make it

four of you, sitting round this table. Then there is someone else you know and care for.'

'That is what the poem says,' Karoline told him cau-
tiously. 'You may read it for yourself if you like.'

She handed him the verses, dashingly written over
two whole sheets. 'So much waste! The back of the paper
not used!'

'He always writes like that.'

'Did you think I was in love with Hardenberg?'

'God forgive me, I did,' Erasmus said at last. 'He has
spoken of you so often. I expect I admire my brother
too much. I deceive myself into thinking that everyone
must feel about him in the same way. I am truly glad I
was wrong – but we both continue, don't we, to feel the
same about – you mustn't think I would be unjust to a
young girl, and you must understand that although I
have always shared Fritz's life I have also known that the
time must come when I will lose the greater half of him,
and I have always hoped that when that time comes I
shall have strength enough to content myself with what's
left for me – but Karoline, disappointment must have its
limits – we continue, surely, to feel the same about –'

Karoline covered her face with her hands. 'How could
he? How could he?'

28

From Sophie's Diary, 1795

January 8

Today once again we were alone and nothing much happened.

January 9

Today we were again alone and nothing much happened.

January 10

Hardenburch came at mid-day.

January 13

Today Hardenburch went away and I had nothing to amuse me.

March 8

Today we all decided to go to church but the weather held us up.

March 11

Today we were all alone and nothing much happened.

March 12

Today was like yesterday and nothing much happened.

March 13

It was a day of penance and Hartenb. was there.

March 14

Today Hartenber. was there he got a letter from his
brother.

29

A Second Reading

THE 17th of March, 1795 was Sophie's 13th birthday. Two days earlier she had promised Fritz that she would marry him.

On the 16th of June the always obliging Karl sent a pair of gold rings from Lützen (where he was stationed) to his brother in Tennstedt.

On the 21st of August he wrote again from Lützen, where, he said, he had been 'vegetating' since the Peace of Basle. 'I am sending the stirrup with its leather, and both the straw hats, on one of which I have left the ribbon, which is the latest fashion. The other one can be worn according to taste.' One was for Erasmus to give to Karoline, one was for Sophie; the distribution was left to Fritz. There was also a workbox for the Mother, and, for the second time, Fritz's gold ring, which had been sent back to Lützen and had now been engraved, as he had asked, with an S. This could not have been done by a jeweller in Tennstedt – a place so small that they evidently didn't know the fashion in straw hats, and indeed had no straw hats to sell – and certainly not in Weissenfels, where it would have caused notice and comment. The Freiherr von Hardenberg had not even been asked for his permission. The very name of Sophie von Kühn had not been mentioned to him.

The Rockenthiens, on the other hand, had scarcely needed to be asked. They were overjoyed, in the first place, simply by the new happiness in the house. Fritz was asked to be little Günther's godfather. George told him that if he was thinking of marrying it would be absolutely necessary for him to buy a new horse. The Gaul could go for cats' meat.

The Hausherr, rather surprisingly, seemed to take no offence at the idea that the Rockenthiens might be thought not good enough for the Hardenbergs. 'She is too young to marry as yet. I do not know even if her periods are regularly established. By the time she is fifteen, we shall find a way out of our difficulties.' Fritz had thought that Coelestin Just, his father's good friend, might be let into their confidence and act as a kind of emissary between Weissenfels and Grüningen. 'Oh, I think that wouldn't serve,' Herr Rockenthien said amiably. 'The Kreisamtmann, as you probably noticed, thinks of me as a fool.'

Almost as soon as he had offered Sophie her ring, and seen her – since she could not wear it openly – hang it round her neck, Fritz asked if he might read her the opening chapter of *The Blue Flower*. 'It is the introduction,' he told her, 'to a story which I cannot write as yet. I do not know even what it will be. I have made a list of occupations and professions, and of psychological types. But perhaps after all it will not be a novel. There is more truth, perhaps, in folktales.'

'Well, I like those,' said Sophie, 'but not if people are to be turned into toads, for that's not amusing.'

'I shall read my introduction aloud, and you must tell me what it means.' Sophie evidently felt weighed down by this responsibility.

'Do you not know yourself?' she asked doubtfully.

'Sometimes I think I do.'

'But has no-one else read it?'

Fritz searched his memory.

'Yes, Karoline Just.'

'Ah, she is clever.'

The Mandelsloh came in, said that she too would listen and handed Sophie her day's sewing. Even in this prosperous household they were turning the sheets and pillow slips sides to middle, which meant that they would last another ten years. Sophie was diverted for a moment by her needle-case. — 'You gave me this, dear Hardenberg!' — but then fell silent.

'His father and mother were already in bed and asleep, the clock on the wall ticked with a monotonous beat, the wind whistled outside the rattling window-pane. From time to time the room grew brighter when the moonlight shone in. The young man lay restlessly on his bed and remembered the stranger and his stories. "It was not the thought of the treasure which stirred up such unspeakable longings in me," he said to himself. "I have no craving to be rich, but I long to see the Blue Flower. It lies incessantly at my heart, and I can imagine and think about nothing else. Never did I feel like this before. It is as if until now I had been dreaming, or as if sleep had carried me into another world. For in the world I used to live in, who would have troubled himself about flowers? Such a wild passion for a flower was never heard of there. But where could this stranger have come from? None of us had ever seen such a man before. And yet I don't know how it was that I alone was truly caught and held by what he told us. Everyone else heard what I did, and yet none of them paid him serious attention."'

Not sure how much more he was going to read, the two women sat without speaking, with their sewing on their laps. Sophie was pale, her mouth was pale rose. There was the gentlest possible gradation between the colour of the face and the slightly open, soft, fresh, full, pale mouth. It was as if nothing had reached, as yet, its proper colour or its full strength — always excepting her dark hair.

The Mandelsloh, who had given the reading her

serious attention, said, 'This is only the beginning of the story. How will it end?'

'I should like you to tell me that,' Fritz answered.

'So far, it is a story for children.'

'That is not against it,' cried Sophie.

'Why do you think this young man can't sleep?' he asked her urgently. 'Is it the moon? Is it the ticking of the clock?'

'Oh, no, that doesn't keep him awake. He only notices it because he is not asleep.'

'That is true,' said the Mandelsloh.

'But would he have slept well, if the stranger had not talked about the Blue Flower?'

'Why should he care about a flower?' Sophie asked. 'He is not a woman, and he is not a gardener.'

'Oh, because it is blue, and he has never seen such a thing,' said the Mandelsloh. 'Flax, I suppose, yes, and linseed, yes, and forget-me-nots and cornflowers, but they are commonplace and have nothing to do with the matter, the Blue Flower is something quite other.'

'Please, Hardenberg, what is the name of the flower?' asked Sophie.

'He knew once,' said Fritz. 'He was told the name, but he has forgotten it. He would give his life to remember it.'

'He can't sleep, because he is alone,' continued the Mandelsloh.

'But there are many in the house,' said Sophie.

'But he is alone in his room. He looks for another dear head on the pillow.'

'Do you agree?' asked Fritz, turning towards Sophie.

'Certainly I should like to know what is going to happen,' she said doubtfully.

He said, 'If a story begins with finding, it must end with searching.'

Sophie did not possess many books. She had her hymnal, her Evangelium, and a list, bound with ribbon, of all the dogs that her family had ever had, although some of them had died so long ago that she could not remember them. To this she now added the introductory chapter of the story of the Blue Flower. This was in the handwriting of Karoline Just, who did all Fritz's copying for him.

'Söphgen likes listening to stories,' Fritz wrote in his notebook. 'She doesn't want to be embarrassed by my love. My love weighs down on her so often. She cares more about other people and their feelings than about her own. But she is cold through and through.'

'What I have written down about her does not make sense,' he said to the Mandelsloh. 'One thing contradicts another. I am going to ask you to write a description of her, as you have known her all her life – a portrait of her, as a sister sees her.'

'Not possible!' said the Mandelsloh.

'I am asking too much of you?'

'Very much too much.'

'Do you never keep a journal?' he asked her.

'What if I do? You keep a diary, but could you describe your brother Erasmus?'

'He describes himself,' said Fritz. His distress remained. There was not even a passable likeness of Sophie in the house, except for a wretched miniature, in which her eyes appeared to bulge like gooseberries, or like Fichte's. Only the hair, falling defiantly over her white muslin dress, was worth looking at. The miniature caused the whole family, Sophie above all, to laugh immoderately.

Fritz asked the Hausherr whether he might find a portrait painter to come to the house, at his expense, to make a likeness of Sophie as she really was. It would be necessary for him to stay a few days to make sketches, but the portrait could be finished in the studio.

'I daresay it will turn out, after all, to be at *my* expense,' said Rockenthien that night to his wife. 'I am not sure that, at the moment, Hardenberg is earning anything.' He himself had never earned anything either, except for his irregularly paid wages as an infantry captain. But he was of course securely married to a wife with a very good property of her own.

30

Sophie's Likeness

FRITZ wanted to find a young painter. He wanted one who painted from the heart, and he settled on Joseph Hoffmann from Köln, who had been recommended to him by Severin.

Hoffmann arrived at Grüningen in late summer, when the roads and the evening light were still good, carrying his knapsack, his necessary, his valise, brushes and port-folio. His fee was to be six thaler, which Fritz intended to meet by selling some of his books. Fritz himself was not at Grüningen, having set himself to work immoder-ately hard, though he intended to come as soon as poss-ible. The painter was late, because the diligence was late. The Rockenthien family were already at table. All were introduced, but it had not occurred to them to wait for him.

The servants had already brought in the soups, one made of beer, sugar and eggs, one of rose-hips and onions, one of bread and cabbage-water, one of cows' udders flavoured with nutmeg. There was dough mixed with beech-nut oil, pickled herrings and goose with treacle sauce, hard-boiled eggs, numerous dumplings. It is dangerous – on this, at least, all Germany's physicians were agreed – not to keep the stomach full at all times.

Good appetite!

A towering Alp of boiled potatoes, trailing long drifts of steam, was placed in the exact centre of the table, so that all might spear away at it with outstretched silver forks. Rapidly, as though in an avalanche, it subsided into ruin.

'I don't want you to look at me now, Herr Maler,' Sophie called across the table. 'Don't study me now, I am about to fill my mouth.'

'Gracious Fräulein, never would I do such a thing in the first few minutes of acquaintance,' said Hoffmann quietly. 'All I am doing is glancing round the table and assessing the presence, or absence, of true soul in the countenance of everyone here.'

'Ach Gott, I should not think you are often asked out to dinner twice,' said the Mandelsloh.

'I will offer you some advice,' said Herr Rockenthien, leaning forward to help himself to potatoes. 'That is my elder stepdaughter. Don't answer her, if what she says offends you.'

'Why should it offend me? I think that the Frau Leutnant is very probably not used to artists.'

'We know Hardenberg,' said the Mandelsloh. 'He is a

poet, which is much the same as an artist. It is true that
we are not quite used to him yet.'

Both the Hausherr and his wife were 'from the land'.
They were country people. The painter Joseph Hoffmann
had been born and brought up in a back street of Köln.
His father had been a ladies' shoemaker who had taken
to drink and lost any skill he once possessed. Hoffmann
had come to the Dresden Academy as a very poor student
and was not much more than that now, making a living
by selling sepia drawings of distant prospects and bends
in the river with reliably grazing cattle. After his sorties
into the country he would hurry back to the reassuring
close greasy pressure of his home town. Here at Schloss
Grüningen he felt a foreigner. He could not eat these
vast quantities, he had never formed the habit, and he
could not make out who most of the people at table
were. But he did not allow this to disconcert him. This
is my time, he thought, and I shall seize my chance. The
world will see what I can do.

He had determined to paint Fräulein Sophie standing
in the sunshine, just at the end of childhood and on the
verge of a woman's joy and fulfilment, and to include
in his portrait the Mandelsloh, her sister, the soldier's
wife, likely to be widowed, sitting in shadow, the victim
of woman's lot. He intended to ask them to pose for him
near one of the many small wayside monuments, put
up to the memory of local landlords and benefactors,

which he had noticed on the way to Grüningen. They acted as landmarks and were used as scratching-posts by the cattle. The lettering on the monument would be seen, but, because of the way the light fell, not clearly. The pressure of these ideas, which urged themselves upon him with the force of poetry, caused him to lay down his knife and fork and to say distinctly, without the least reference to the loud voices around him.

'Yes, there, exactly there.'

'Where?' asked Frau Rockenthien, who saw him by now as one more object for compassion.

'I should like to paint your two daughters near a fountain – sitting on stone steps – broken, time-worn stone. In the distance, a glimpse of the sea.'

'We are some way from the sea,' said Rockenthien doubtfully. 'I would say about a hundred and eighty miles. Strategically, that will always be one of our problems.'

'Strategy does not interest me,' said the young painter. 'Bloodshed does not interest me. Apart from that, what does the sea suggest to you?'

But to no-one present did it suggest anything, except salt water. Indeed none of them, except Rockenthien, who had once been stationed with the Hanoverian Regiment at Ratzeburg, had ever seen it.

Frau Rockenthien said peaceably that when she was

young, sea air had been thought very unhealthy, but she was not quite sure what doctors said about it nowadays.

31

I Could Not Paint Her

THE whole household wondered how Sophie was to be kept sitting still for the necessary length of time. The miniaturist, an elderly relative, had not required her to keep still at all, but had made do with tracing her shadow on a piece of white pasteboard. Hoffmann, however, made only a few sketches on the wing – Fräulein von Kühn running, Fräulein von Kühn pouring milk from a jug. He appeared, after this, to go into a kind of trance, and spent much time in his room.

'Heartily I wish Hardenberg were here,' said Rockenthien. 'This painter is welcome among us, and I thought we had done pretty well in giving him one of the top-floor drying rooms for a studio, but I can't say that he seems at home. The women, however, must manage these things.' By 'the women' he meant, of course, the Mandelsloh, but she had little patience with Hoffmann. 'He has been trained, I suppose, as a cobbler is trained to mend shoes, or a soldier to shoot his enemies. Let him take out his pencils and brushes, and set to.'

'Yes, but perhaps he can't get a likeness,' said Rocken-thien. 'It's a trick, you know. You can't learn it, you're born with it. That's how these fellows — Dürer, Raphael, all those fellows — that's how they made their money.'

'I don't think that so far Hoffmann has made much money,' said the Mandelsloh doubtfully.

'Again, that's the trick of it. They have much more money than they let on, that's to say, if they can get a likeness.'

Sophie was sorry for Hoffmann, and the instinct to console which she inherited from her mother led her to ask to see all the drawings which he had brought with him in his portfolio and to praise everything in turn, and indeed she did consider them as marvels. Finally Hoffmann sighed. 'You, too, have studied drawing, I am sure, gracious Fräulein. You must show me what you have done.'

'No, that I won't do,' said Sophie. 'As soon as the drawing-master was gone, I tore them all up.'

She is not such a fool, thought Hoffmann.

Sophie's Diary:

Tuesday September 11
Today the painter did not come down in the morn-ing for breakfast. My stepmother sent up one of the

menservants with his coffee, but he said through the door, namely that he wished to be allowed to think.

Wednesday September 12

We began pickling the raspberries.

Thursday September 13

Today was hot and there was thunder and nothing happened and Hardenburch did not come.

Friday September 14

Today no-one came and nothing happened.

Saturday September 15

The painter did not come downstairs, to drink schnaps with us.

Sunday September 16

The painter did not come to the Lord's service with us.

Monday September 17

My stepfather said, is that painter fellow still upstairs, let us hope he has not got any of the maids to bed with him.

Anxious to see whether this was the case, George commandeered a ladder from the stables and propped it against the painter's window, open to catch what breeze there was. Such a thing would have been impossible to imagine at Weissenfels. On the other hand George, unlike the Bernhard, would never have gone through a visitor's luggage.

A stable lad was told to hold the ladder steady, and

George shinned up. 'Do you see anything?' bawled the lad, with whom George shared most of his activities.

'I'm not sure, it's dark inside. Hang on, Hansel, I think I can hear the bedsprings creaking.'

But Hansel lost his nerve and did not hang on. The ladder toppled sideways, slowly at first, then sickeningly faster. George, bellowing for help, had the sense to jump clear, but fell with the back of his head on the flagstones. The brass buttons on the tails of his jacket rang against the stones, and a moment later his head struck them grossly, like an unwanted parcel. He was lucky only to break a collar-bone, but was not present when the painter, on the next day, left Schloss Grüningen.

Waiting forlornly in the vestibule, Hoffmann, again with his valise, portfolio, brushes, and necessary, was seen off with genuine kindness by Rockenthien, who said, 'I am sorry you have not found it possible to do more, Herr Maler. You must allow me to recompense you for the time you have spent.'

'No, no, my commission was from Hardenberg, and I shall explain myself to him. In any case,' he added firmly, 'you must not think I am without resources.'

This confirmed Rockenthien in his conviction that painters knew a trick or two, and he felt less uneasy. 'I am sorry you had to stay so much upstairs. But they sent up whatever you wanted, eh? They fed you, eh?'

'I have received every hospitality,' said Hoffmann. 'I should like to wish Master George a rapid recovery.'

George was soon up and about, but furious that while he had been laid up, Hansel had been given a good beating by the head coachman, and was to be dismissed. Against the head coachman's decisions nobody, and certainly not the Hausherr, dared to make any representation. 'There is no justice in this house,' George cried. 'This artist had failed entirely to paint my sister, and yet he receives nothing but compliments. As for Hansel, he only did what he was told.'

'No-one told him to let go of the ladder,' said the Hausherr.

Weissenfels was on Hoffmann's road back to Dresden. Although he never took much to drink, he felt by that time in need of a stimulant, and when the diligence halted he got down and went into the Wilde Mann, where he found Fritz.

This is not what I wanted, he thought, and yet I must explain myself at some time. Fritz threw his arms round him. 'The portrait-painter!'

'I came here because I thought that if you were in Weissenfels at all, you would be at your house, and I could not face meeting you.'

'Don't look so wretched, Hoffmann. I have already had a note from Sophie herself, no less, and I know that you have not finished the portrait or even begun it. Shall I send out for schnaps?'

'No, no, a glass of plain beer, if you are so good.' Hoffmann never took anything strong, fearing to follow the same road as his father.

'Well, let us talk. You have surely made sketches?'

'I have, and they are yours if you want them, but I am not satisfied.'

'Evidently it can't be easy to draw my Sophie. But do you know the engraving from Raphael's self-portrait in the third volume of Lavater's *Physiognomie*?'

'Yes, I know it.'

'And do you not think that the Raphael is the image of my Sophie?'

'No,' said Hoffmann. 'Except for the eyes, which are dark in both cases, there is very little resemblance.' His mind became steadier as he sipped at the dreary *Einfaches*, which resembled the water in which beans have been cooked.

'Hardenberg, I hope you do not doubt my skill. I received eight years' training in Dresden before I was even admitted to the life class. But the truth is that I have been defeated by Fräulein von Kühn. At first I was concerned with the setting – the background – but very soon that no longer mattered to me. It was the gracious Fräulein who puzzled me.'

'The artist's feeling justifies him,' said Fritz. 'That must always be true, for art and nature follow the same laws.'

'That is so. Pure sensations can never be in contradiction to nature. Never!'

'I don't altogether understand Söphgen myself,' Fritz went on. 'That is why I required a good portrait of her. But perhaps we shouldn't have expected that you —'

'Oh, I can see at once what she is,' Hoffmann broke out recklessly. 'A decent, good-hearted Saxon girl, potato-fed, with the bloom of thirteen summers, and the coarser glow of thirteen winters.' He overrode whatever protest it was that Fritz had begun, or rather he ignored it in the intensity of his wish to be understood. 'Hardenberg, in every created thing, whether it is alive or whether it is what we usually call inanimate, there is an attempt to communicate, even among the totally silent. There is a question being asked, a different question for every entity, which for the most part will never be put into words, even by those who can speak. It is asked incessantly, most of the time however hardly noticeably, even faintly, like a church bell heard across meadows and enclosures. Best for the painter, once having looked, to shut his eyes, his physical eyes though not those of the spirit, so that he may hear it more distinctly. You must have listened for it, Hardenberg, for Fräulein Sophie's question, you must have strained to make it out, even though, as I think very probable, she does not know herself what it is.'

'I am trying to understand you,' said Fritz.

Hoffmann had put his hand to his ear, a very curious gesture for a young man.

'I could not hear her question, and so I could not paint.'

32

The Way Leads Inwards

FRITZ did not risk taking the painter to the Kloster Gasse, where he would surely say something to his parents about Sophie. There was no alternative to seeing him off from the Wilde Mann when the diligence left for Köln.

He did not want to go straight home, but walked a little way out of the town and into a churchyard which he knew well. It was by now the very late afternoon, pale blue above clear yellow, with the burning clarity of the northern skies, growing more and more transparent, as though to end in revelation.

The entrance to the churchyard was a large iron gate, with gilt letters on it, intertwined. The municipality of Weissenfels had intended to run to an iron fence as well, but at the moment the gate was set in wooden palings which more or less served to keep the cows in the pastor's front yard away from the graves. Knee-deep in the presbytery dung-heap they watched the passers-by without curiosity. Fritz walked among the grass mounds which were now, with the green alleys between them, almost disappearing in the rising mist. As in most graveyards, there were a number of objects left lying about – an iron ladder, a dinner basket and even a spade, as though work here were always in progress, and always liable to be interrupted. The crosses, iron and stone, appeared to grow out of the earth, the smaller ones struggling to get as tall as the others. Some had fallen. You could not say that the churchyard, which was a place for family walks on public holidays, was neglected, but neither was it well kept. There were weeds and a few geese. Stinging insects from the dungheaps and from God's acre joined in triumphant clouds in the strong sickly air.

The creak and thump of the pastor's cows could still be heard far into the burial ground where the graves and the still empty spaces, cut off from each other now by the mist, had become dark green islands, dark green chambers of meditation. On one of them, just a little ahead of him, a young man, still almost a boy, was standing in the half darkness, with his head bent, himself as white, still, and speechless as a memorial. The sight was consoling to Fritz, who knew that the young man, although living, was not human, but also that at the moment there was no boundary between them.

He said aloud, 'The external world is the world of shadows. It throws its shadows into the kingdom of light. How different they will appear when this darkness is gone and the shadow-body has passed away. The universe, after all, is within us. The way leads inwards, always inwards.'

When he got back to the Kloster Gasse, with the impulse to tell somebody about what he had seen, Sidonie immediately asked him who was that man who had been talking to him with so much feeling at the Wilde Mann — Gottfried had seen them — Oh, so it was the poor painter! — Why poor? Fritz asked — Gottfried had given it as his opinion that there were tears in his eyes. Well, Erasmus asked, has he done the portrait? No, Fritz said, he has not been successful. He had done his best to forgive Erasmus. They never, in the ordinary way of things, discussed Sophie. He regarded his brother as an obstinate heathen.

'Are there no sketches?' Sidonie asked.

'Yes, a few,' Fritz told her. 'But they are a kind of notation only — a few lines, a cloud of hair. He declares she is undrawable. What distresses me is my ring, for it was to have a smaller version of the portrait inside it, when it was ready. Now I must content myself with that misbegotten miniature.'

'You can't leave that ring alone,' said the Bernhard, who had come in, silent-footed, from school. 'Always engraved and re-engraved. It would be much better plain.'

'You have never seen it,' said Sidonie. 'None of us has ever seen it.' She smiled at her eldest brother. 'I daresay after all that you are not sorry to think that your Sophie is undrawable.'

Sidonie was making anxious calculations about Gottfried. He might be asked about the stranger in the Wilde Mann, and it would be impossible for him, if asked, to do anything less than tell the truth to the Freiherr. But then, Gottfried did not know that the man he had seen was a painter, and Sidonie was reassured also by the thought that her father never gave his concentrated attention to more than one subject at a time. Lately, to her mother's relief, he had once again allowed the *Leipziger Zeitung* into the house. At the moment he was anxious to hear how much Fritz had gathered from his visit to the salt-works and pan-houses of Artern, then he wished to discuss, or rather to give his opinions, on Buonaparte, who, on the whole, he thought, showed signs of competence. That should last them at least until tomorrow.

Fritz went in through the shabby darkly-polished house, where the sound of the early evening hymn-singing could be heard from behind the shut doors of the kitchen quarters. First to his mother and little Christoph, thin as a shadow with summer fever. 'Are you well, Fritz? Is there anything you want? Are you happy?' He would have liked to ask her to give him something, or to tell him something, but could think of nothing. She asked unexpectedly, 'Are you concealing anything from your father?' Fritz took her hand. 'You must trust me, mother! I shall tell him everything — that is, everything that —' With quite unaccustomed energy she cried, 'No, in heaven's name, whatever it is, don't do that!'

33

At Jena

BEFORE starting work in earnest, but having realised at Artern what it would be like when he did, Fritz went to see his friends at Jena. The Gaul could do the necessary thirty miles, though without enthusiasm. He had not been to see them, Caroline Schlegel had been saying, for centuries.

'We shall hope to hear him talking, as he used to do, before he gets round the corner of Grammatische Strasse,' said Dorothea Schlegel, 'saying something about the Absolute.'

Johann Wilhelm Ritter, a guest in her house as so often, reminded her that Hardenberg could not be judged by any ordinary standards, not even the ordinary standards of Jena, where fifteen out of every twenty inhabitants were said to be Professors. 'For him there is no real barrier between the unseen and the seen. The whole of existence dissolves itself into a myth.'

'But that is the trouble,' interrupted Caroline. 'He used, of course, to say that every day the world was drawing nearer to infinity. Now, we are told, he interests himself in the extraction and refinement of salt and brown coal, which can't be dissolved into a myth, no matter how hard he tries.'

'Goethe himself undertook to administer a silver mine for the Duke of Saxe-Weimar,' said her husband.

'Very unsuccessfully. Goethe's mine went bankrupt. However, I believe that Hardenberg will manage his efficiently, and that is what I can't forgive him. *Enfin*, he will become totally *merkantilistisch*. He will marry the niece of the Kreisamtmann and in good time he will become a Kreisamtmann himself.'

'I am sorry that he allows himself to become an object of jest,' said Ritter.

'That is not on account of his philosophy, or even his mania for salt. It is because he has such large hands and feet,' said Caroline. 'We all love him.'

'Dearly we love him,' said Dorothea.

In Jena, in autumn, friends walked together in the pine woods above the little town, or in Paradise, Jena's name for its towpath along the Saale. Sometimes Goethe, who often spent the summers here, was to be seen in Paradise, also walking, his hands clasped behind his back, in reverie. He was now forty-six years old, and was referred to by the Schlegel women as His Ancient and Divine Majesty. Goethe did not like to meet too many people at once.

As he advanced, groups dexterously broke up before he was obliged to meet them. Fritz hung back, not aspiring to the attention of so great a man.

'And yet you have plenty to say,' Caroline told him. 'You could speak to him, as a young man, a coming poet, to one who seems almost indestructible.'

'I have nothing good enough to show him.'

'Never mind,' she said. 'You may talk to me, Hardenberg. Talk to me about salt.'

The musical evenings and *conversazione* at Jena were crowded, but not everyone said brilliant things, or indeed, anything at all. Some of the guests stood uneasily, certain that they had been invited, but not, now that they had arrived, that their names had been remembered.

'Dietmahler!'

'Hardenberg! I knew you as soon as you came into the room.'

'How do I come into a room?'

Dietmahler scarcely liked to say, You still look ridiculous and everyone is still glad to see you. He felt, like a wound, the irrecoverable gap between student days and those that follow.

'Are you a surgeon now?' Fritz asked him.

'Not quite, but soon. You see I have not moved far from Jena. When I qualify, I shall not do so badly. My mother is alive, but I have no younger brothers now and no sisters.'

'*Gott sei Dank*, I have plenty of both,' cried Fritz, on an impulse. 'Come and stay with us in Weissenfels. Dear friend, pay us a visit.'

It was in this way that Dietmahler witnessed the Great Wash at Weissenfels, and told the Freiherr von Hardenberg, in all sincerity, that he knew nothing about his son's entanglement with a young woman of the middle class, or, indeed, with any other woman.

34

The Garden-House

AT Tennstedt, Karoline Just heard that the Rockenthiens had asked Fritz to stand godfather to Günther, the new baby. She thought, 'They are trying to bind him to them with links of iron.'

Erasmus, who wrote to her from Hubertusberg, was her only ally. 'I am prepared to resign myself, as I explained to you, to taking a much smaller place in Fritz's life,' he told her, 'at least, I tell myself that I am resigned. But not to having him taken away from us by a greedy infant. If Sophie von Kühn is an infant, however, by the way, she will not stay constant, she will change her mind. And yet I don't quite like the idea of that either.'

Fritz came back to Tennstedt, and went into the kitchen, saying he was too dusty from the summer's roads for the front room. 'Where is the Kreisamtmann? Where is Frau Rahel?'

What does it matter where they are? Karoline felt like answering. You have been away for so long, now is your opportunity to speak to someone who truly understands you. Didn't you say that we were like two watches, set to the same time? She said aloud, 'They are in their garden-house. Yes! It is finished at last.'

'That I must see,' said Fritz. He was washing his face and hands under the pump, but as she put on her shawl he added, in a voice of great tenderness, 'Dear Justen, you must not think I have forgotten the things we talked about not so long ago.' Karoline did think he had forgotten all or most of it. Then as he dried himself he repeated, 'Never does the heart sigh in vain, Justen,' and she scarcely knew whether to be unhappy or not. In her mouth was something bitter, that tasted like the waters of death.

She would have twenty minutes alone with him on the walk down to the garden, which was in an area on the outskirts called the Runde. He would give her his arm. But they would have to stop and talk on the way to many neighbours and acquaintances, all of whom would say: 'Ah, Freiherr, so you are back from Jena.' 'Yes, back from Jena.' 'We are glad that your health has been spared, we are glad to see you back from Jena.' Many of these people would get up in Tennstedt, and go to bed again there at the end of the day, perhaps in all eighteen thousand or so times.

'How good it is to be alive,' several of them said, 'in this warm weather.'

The Justs' plot was small, and had no trees, but they

had bought it already cultivated and it was planted up with vegetables, honeysuckle and centifolia roses. The garden-house itself was one of an accepted pattern, which could be ordered from either of the two master carpenters in Tennstedt, and was handsomely framed in carved and gilded wood. Its name was conspicuous, *Der Garten Eden*.

The Justs sat in a cloud of smoke from the Kreis-amtmann's pipe, side by side on a new bench at the new entrance. There was no room for anyone else. This, too, was part of the accepted design of a garden-house. They looked happily outwards towards the Runde, half-asphyxiated by the fragrance of hop-vines, honeysuckle and tobacco. 'Hail, ever-blessed pair!' cried Fritz, from a distance.

Just, as he himself very well knew, had lately become almost absurdly absorbed by the details of design and installation. He had taken Fritz to Artern, as part of his apprenticeship, to listen to both sides in a disagreement between the different brotherhoods of salt workers. But although he had told Fritz to take careful notes, he had returned with impatience to the matter of the exact placing of the *Vorbau*, or porch, on the garden-house. At what angle would it receive most morning sun? After-noon sun, of course, was to be avoided.

Even now, while Rahel was asking after her former friends in Jena (but without, Fritz thought, her old hint of sharpness), the Kreisamtmann once again introduced the subject of the *Vorbau*. It had always seemed to Fritz that Coelestin Just knew what contentment was, but not passion, and could therefore be accounted a happy man. He saw now how mistaken he had been. It was discontent that, at last, was making Just truly happy. Although, short of dismantling and re-constructing the entire garden-house nothing could now be done about the *Vorbau*, he would never be quite satisfied with it, never cease to build and rebuild it in his mind. The universe, after all, is within us.

35

Sophie is Cold Through and Through

Sophie to Fritz — '. . . I have coughs and sneezes, but it seems to me that I feel quite well again when you are in my mind. Your Sophie.'

In the autumn of 1795 Fritz plodded over to Grüningen to find Sophie without cares. She was playing with Günther, whose experience of life must so far have been favourable, since he smiled at anything in human form. 'He is stronger by far than our Christoph,' said Fritz with a pang of regret. Günther did nothing by halves. He had caught the household's cough, but reserved it for the night-time, when it echoed, like a large dog barking, down the corridors.

'Yes, he smiles and coughs at us all alike,' said Fritz, 'and yet I'm flattered when my turn comes. It is so much more pleasant to deceive oneself.'

'Hardenberg, why have you not written to me?' Sophie asked.

'Dear, dear Söphgen, I wrote to you every day this

week. On Monday I wrote to explain to you that although God created the world it has no real existence until we apprehend it.'

'So all this unholy muddle is our own doing,' said the Mandelsloh. 'What a thing to tell a young girl!'

'Things of the body aren't our own doing,' said Sophie. 'I have a pain in my left side, and that is not my own doing.'

'Well, let us all complain to each other,' said Fritz, but the Mandelsloh declared that she was always well. 'Did you not know that? It is generally agreed that I was born to be always well. My husband is quite sure of it, and so is everyone in this house.'

'Why did you not come earlier, Hardenburch?' asked Sophie.

'I have to work very seriously now,' he told her. 'If we are ever to get married, I must apply myself. I sit up late at night, reading.'

'But why do you do all this reading? You are not a student any more.'

'He would not read if he was,' said the Mandelsloh. 'Students do not read, they drink.'

'Why do they drink?' Sophie asked.

'Because they desire to know the whole truth,' said Fritz, 'and that makes them desperate.'

Günther, who had been half asleep, came to, and protested.

'What would it cost them,' Sophie asked, 'to know the whole truth?'

'They can't reckon that,' said Fritz, 'but they know they can get drunk for three groschen.'

She is thirteen, she will be fourteen, fifteen, sixteen. It takes time. One would say that God has stopped his clock.

But she is cold, cold through and through.

36

Dr Hofrat Ebhard

A T Grüningen, when Fritz was gone, the Mandelsloh asked
why Sophie had mentioned the pain in her left side. 'You
told me we were not to say anything about it.'

'He is not to know,' said Sophie earnestly.

'Then why did you speak of it?'

'Just for the pleasure of talking about it while he was
there. He took no notice, you know, Frieke, I laughed
and so he did not notice it.'

The pain was no better by the beginning of November.
It was Sophie's first serious illness, the first illness in fact
that she had ever had. At first they thought it better not
to notify Fritz, but on the 14th of November, when he
went back to the Justs' house at mid-day, the maid Christel, when she brought him his coffee, told him that there
was a messenger waiting for him. The messenger was
from Grüningen. Christel's feelings about this were
mixed, for she wanted at all costs to keep the young
Freiherr in the house. He had come to them, and she
considered him theirs, and indeed hers.

'I was not too frightened at first,' Fritz wrote to Karl, 'but when I heard that she was ill – my Philosophy was ill – I notified Just (we had been starting on the year's accounts) and without any further enquiry left for Grüningen.'

'What am I to tell Fräulein Karoline?' Christel had asked. 'She has gone to the market.'

'Tell her what you told me, she will feel exactly the same as I do,' he had said.

Sophie's pain was the first symptom of a tumour on her hip related to tuberculosis. Such pains can disappear, it is said, of their own accord. The doctor, Hofrat Friedrich Ebhard, relied a good deal on this possibility, and a good deal on experience. Of Brownismus he had never had the opportunity to learn anything.

In his *Elementa Medicinae* Brown gives a Table of Excitability for the main disorders, the correct balance being indicated by the figure 40. Phthisis, the early stage of consumption, is shown in his table as coming well below 40. Brown, therefore, in cases of phthisis, would prescribe that the wish to go on living should be supported by electric shocks, alcohol, camphor and rich soups.

None of these things suggested themselves to Ebhard, but he made no mistake in his diagnosis. This was not surprising, since one in four of his patients died of consumption. Fräulein von Kühn was young, but youth in these cases was not always on the patient's side. He had never had the chance to hear the opening of *The Blue Flower*, but if he had done so he could have said immediately what he thought it meant.

37

What is Pain?

SOPHIE's cough soon put Günther's into the shade. It came with an immense draught of breath which reminded her of laughing, so that in fact she would have been hard put to it, except for the pain, not to laugh.

What if there were no such thing as pain? When they were all children at Grüningen, Friederike, not yet the Mandelsloh, but already on duty, used to collect them together after the evening service to tell them a Sunday story.

'There was a certain honest shopkeeper,' she said, 'who unlike the rest of us, felt no pain. He had never felt any since he was born, so that when he reached the age of forty-five he was quite unaware that he was ill and never thought to call the doctor, until one night he heard the sound of the door opening, and sitting up in his bed saw in the bright moonlight that someone he did not know had come into his room, and that this was Death.'

Sophie had been unable to grasp the point of the story.

'He was so lucky, Frieke.'

'Not at all. The pain would have been a warning to him that he was ill, and as it was he had no warning.'

'We don't want any warnings,' the children told her. 'We get into enough trouble as it is.'

'But he had no time to consider how he had spent his life, and to repent.'

'Repentance is for old women and arse-holes,' shouted George.

'George, no-one can tolerate you,' said Friederike. 'They ought to whip you at school.'

'They do whip me at school,' said George.

The Hofrat ordered the application of linseed poultices to Sophie's hip, which were so scalding hot that they marked the skin for good. The linseed smelled of the open forest, of solid furniture, of the night-watchman's heavy oiled boots, specially issued to him by the town councillors because he had to patrol the streets in all weathers, of pine trees and green spruce. Unmistakeably, Sophie began to get better.

'*Liebster, bester Freund*,' Rockenthien wrote to Fritz. 'How are you? Here it is the same old story. Söphgen dances, jumps, sings, demands to be taken to the fair at Greussen, eats like a woodcutter, sleeps like a rat, walks straight as a fir-tree, has given up whey and medicine, has to take two baths a day by way of treatment, and is as happy as a fish in water.'

'Sometimes, I wish that I were the Hausherr,' Fritz wrote to Karl from Tennstedt, 'the world is not a problem to him, and yet this time what he says is true. My dear, treasured Philosophy had had sleepless nights, burning fever, had been bled twice, was too feeble to move. The Hofrat — by the way, it is possible that he is a fool — spoke of inflammation of the liver. And now, since the 20th of November, we are told and indeed we can see with our own eyes that all danger is past.' He asked Karl to send, by a good messenger, two hundred oysters — these to go straight to Grüningen, as a delicacy for the invalid — and to Tennstedt, Fritz's winter trousers, his woollen stockings, his *santés* (the comforters that went under the waistcoat), material for a green jacket, white cashmere for a waistcoat and trousers, a hat, and the loan of Karl's gold epaulettes. He would explain later why he wanted these things, and he would come to Weissenfels and settle up while *der Alte* was meeting old friends, as he did once a year, at the fair in Dresden.

38

Karoline at Grüningen

EVEN Tennstedt had its fair, specialising in *Kesselfleisch* — the ears, snout and strips of fat from the pig's neck boiled with peppermint schnaps. Great iron kettles dispersed the odours of pig sties and peppermint. There was music of sorts, and the stall-keepers, who had come in from the country, danced with each other to keep warm. Karoline had been accustomed to go to the fair at first with her uncle, then with her uncle and step-aunt, and she did so again this year. — A fine young woman still, what a pity she has no affianced to treat her to a pig's nostril!

Her uncle said, 'You will want to call at Schloss Grüningen, to congratulate them on their daughter's renewed health. Why do you not come with me next week, when I have to see Rockenthien on business?'

Karoline had never asked him, and did not now ask, what he thought of Hardenberg's engagement, although he must surely know about it, and how he felt about the Freiherr being kept so long in the dark. She was sure that it must give him pain to conceal anything from his old friend, and in this case the Freiherr had trusted him, after all, to supervise his eldest son. But she knew also that her uncle, like most men, believed that what had not been put into words, and indeed into written words, was not of great importance.

For their visit to the Rockenthiens, Coelestin had hired a horse and trap. They broke their journey at Gebesee, where the manor house belonged, he told Karoline, to the von Oldershausen family – the family, that was, of the Freiherr's long dead first wife. 'The property is now in ruins. They have not been fortunate.'

At the Black Boy, he sent out for schnaps, and looked at his niece attentively for the first time for months, since though he was no less fond of her than ever, her health and well-being could now fairly be left to Rahel. He felt that he should, perhaps, be sorry about something.

'My dear, you must be very tired of hearing about my garden and my garden-house.'

She smiled. That was not the trouble, then, Just thought to himself. Try again. At different ages, women had different troubles, but always there was something. 'I had meant to tell you that in Treffurt, a few weeks ago, I saw your cousin Carl August.'

She gave the same smile.

'And my sister, your Aunt Luisa, and I . . .'

'You thought the two of us might make a respectable

match. But, you know, I haven't seen Carl August for years, and he is younger than I am.'

'One would never think it, Karolinchen. You are always rather pale, but . . .'

Karoline put a lump of sugar and a small amount of hot water in her glass. 'Don't make any arrangements for me with Tante Luisa, Uncle. Wait until all hope is gone, until behind me roars youth's wild ocean.'

'Is that from some poem or other?' asked Just doubtfully.

'Yes, from some poem or other. To tell you the truth, I don't like my cousin.'

'My dear, you said yourself you hadn't seen him for some time. I think I can tell you exactly when.'

In one of the top inside pockets of his winter coat, Just kept his minutely written diary for the last five years, and he began now to pat the outside of his pocket, as though expecting it to call out to him in response.

'My cousin was very irritating then, and he will be very irritating now,' Karoline went on. 'I am sure he prides himself on his consistency.'

'You must not let yourself become too difficult, my Karoline,' said her uncle, in some distress, and she reflected that he was being a little more frank than he had no doubt intended, and that she must not let him worry, as he would probably soon begin to do, that he had hurt her feelings. But it was never difficult to distract him. 'I daresay Hardenberg has spoiled me,' she said. 'I daresay talking to a poet has turned my head.'

At Schloss Grüningen she was relieved to find that Rockenthien had already gone to his office. The Kreis-amtmann followed him there. Karoline paid her respects to the tranquil mistress of the house, and admired Günther, to whom she had sent an ivory teething ring, with a porcelain sweet-box for Sophie, marzipan and *pfefferkuchen* for Mimi and Rudi, and a brace of hares for the household.

'You are a good, generous girl,' said Frau Rockenthien. 'Your lodger, Hardenberg, is here, you know, and his brother Erasmus, yes, Erasmus this time. He often brings one of his brothers with him.'

Karoline's heart seemed to open and shut.

'I expect Hardenberg will return with us to Tennstedt this evening,' she said.

'Ach, well, they are in the morning room now. All are welcome, it is no matter and it is no trouble, whoever comes,' said Frau Rockenthien, and indeed for her it was not. 'I don't know, however, why Hardenberg has sent quite so many oysters. Do you care for oysters, my dear? Of course, they do not keep for ever.'

The morning room. Hardenberg, Erasmus, Friederike Mandelsloh, George trying, apparently for the first time, to play the flute, a pack of little dogs, Sophie in a pale pink dress. When Karoline had last seen her she had thought of her as one of the children. She still thought of her as one of the children. Every night she prayed that she might be spared to have children of her own, though not, perhaps, children quite like Sophie.

Hardenberg stayed beside his Philosophy, with his large feet stowed away under his chair. Erasmus came over at once to Karoline, delighted, not having expected to see her. Sophie was in raptures, absolutely genuine, over her sweet-box; she was going to give up chewing tobacco altogether, only sweets from now on.

'They will give you colic,' said the Mandelsloh.

'Ach, I have colic already. I tell Hardenburch he must call me his little wind-bag.'

Karoline turned to Erasmus, as though to another survivor from drowning. 'This is really all I need,' she thought, 'one moment only with someone who feels as I do.' And Erasmus took her hand in his warm one, and seemed about to say something, but in another moment he had turned back towards Sophie with an indulgent smile, half-senseless, like a drunken man.

Karoline perceived that Erasmus also had fallen in love with Sophie von Kühn.

39

The Quarrel

IN his poem for her thirteenth birthday Fritz wrote that he could hardly credit that there had been a time when he had not known Sophie and when he was 'the man of yesterday,' careless, irresponsible, and so forth. The man of yesterday was now set, once and forever, on the right path. 'But he has been hateful to me,' Sophie told the Mandelsloh, 'we have quarrelled, it is all over.'

This was all the more unjust because she had looked forward to her first quarrel, having been told by her friend, Jette Goldacker, that she and Hardenberg certainly ought to have one. It was the right thing for lovers to do, the Goldacker had said, and afterwards the ties between them would be strengthened. But what can we quarrel about? Sophie asked. About any little thing, it seemed, the more unimportant the better. But after they had been sitting together talking for about half an hour, perhaps not quite so long, her Hardenberg broke out, as though something in him had been overstretched and worked ruinously loose: 'Sophie, you are thirteen years old. How have you spent your time so far? Your first year was passed, I suppose, in smiling and sucking, as little Günther does now. During your second year, as girls are more forward than boys, you learned to speak. Your first words – what were they? "I want!" At three you became still greedier, and finished off the sweet wine from the grown-ups' glasses. At four you began to laugh, and finding that pleasant, you laughed at everything and everybody. At five years old they started to try to educate you. At eleven, having learned nothing, you discovered you had become a woman. You were frightened, I daresay, and went to your gracious mother, who told you not to disturb yourself. Then it came to you that those succulent looks of yours, not quite blonde, not quite brunette, made it unnecessary for you to know, still less to say, anything rational. And now, of course, you're crying, sensibility itself, I suppose, let us see how long you can cry for, my Philosophy –'

He had no manners, Sophie had wept. That was what they said to her when she was in disgrace, the strongest reproach she knew. Fritz replied that he had been to the Universities of Jena, Leipzig and Wittenberg, and knew somewhat more about manners than a thing of thirteen.

'A thing of thirteen, Frieke! Can you believe that, can you explain that?'

'How did he explain it himself?'

'He said I was a torment to him.'

In his next letters to Sophie, Fritz called himself inexcusable, uncultivated, ungracious, impolite, incorrect, intolerable, impertinent and inhuman.

The Mandelsloh advised him to stop it. 'Whatever the cause of the trouble was, she has forgotten it.'

'There was no cause,' Fritz told her.

'That makes it more difficult, still, she has forgotten it.'

He set about applying to Prince Friedrich August III, in Dresden, for consideration as a salaried salt mine inspector designate in the Electorate of Saxony.

40

How to Run a Salt Mine

It was still Fritz's business to take the minutes and pick up what he could, in silence, at the meetings of the Direction Committee, which were held at the Salt Offices in Weissenfels. Freiherr von Hardenberg presided, assisted by Salt Mine Director Bergrath Heun and Salt Mine Inspector Bergrath Senf. The Bernhard delighted in this name – Salt Mine Inspector Mustard! – and he alone – although everybody knew about it – referred openly to the unfortunate episode when, as a result of falsifying the receipts for official building work and sending unauthorised sums on his own private house, Senf had been sentenced to two years in the common convicts' jail, subsequently reduced to eight weeks' normal imprisonment. 'That was a pity,' said the Bernhard. 'We could have chatted to him about it, it would have been interesting to know what it was like to live on bread and water.' 'You may make the experiment here at home, at any time you like,' said Sidonie.

Heun was of a very different character from Senf. Only

a few years older than his two colleagues, he seemed ancient, and referred to himself as 'old Heun, the living archive of the salt mines'. In his long coat of coarse stuff, in which dust seemed to be incorporated, he suggested one of those elementals of the caves and passages of the inner earth, who emerge only reluctantly, and not with good omen, into daylight. The idea partly arose from his blanched skin and frequent blinking and creaking. 'The living archive has, perhaps, a touch of the rheumatismus.' Heun, given time, could answer on every point. He consulted the ledgers only to see that they confirmed the details and figures he had given. 'They would not dare to do otherwise,' thought Fritz.

Senf, on the other hand, smouldered with the suppressed energy of a very intelligent man who, as the result of a foolish miscalculation, was never likely to be able to profit from his intelligence again. At certain fixed intervals everyone connected with the mines and the salt works was permitted to submit their suggestions for improvements in writing. In an elaborate scheme, to which he still hoped his name would be one day attached, Senf had proposed that the salt of Thuringia and Saxony should no longer be evaporated in iron pans over wood fires at eighty degrees centigrade, but by the sun's warmth only. Very many fewer salt workers would be needed and there would be no necessity for them to have houses on the premises. His projects for solar power passed over, Senf put forward a new proposal for doubling the number of wheels on the pulleys which drew the salt water to the surface. 'When the Director, Freiherr von Hardenberg, had considered this scheme,' Fritz wrote in his minutes, 'his comment was, *Quod potest fieri per pauca, non debet fieri per plura* (Manage with as little as you can).' Salt Mine Inspector Senf replied with much warmth that this was not the way forward, and that these mean economies led rather to inertia and stagnation. In any case, with the coming of the nineteenth century, a time when, as Kant had foreseen, men would at last have learned to govern themselves, pulleys and tread wheels would in all probability have no place. Salt Mine Director Heun remarked that in that event, they need not waste more time in discussing them. Inspector Senf said that he was obliged to accept the Director's decision, but could not pretend that he felt satisfied.

'I have applied myself to everything you asked for,' Fritz told his father, 'and I shall do so even more earnestly in the future. You cannot expect me, in a few months, to become like old Heun.'

'Unfortunately I cannot and do not,' said the Freiherr. 'Even if you are granted a long life, I do not think you will ever resemble Wilhelm Heun.'

Formerly when he rode across country Fritz had admired the ancient mountains. Now he looked at the foothills and the coal-bearing ranges with a prospector's

eye for copper, silver, and lignite. He intended to be a
practical engineer and went, as often as he could manage
it, down the shafts of the *Bergwerke*, wearing a miner's
grey jacket and trousers.

'Your son would like to live underground,' Just told
the Freiherr. 'Only reluctantly he returns to the light of
day . . . I warned him, of course, that he must not shake
hands with the miners, as they would consider that it
brought bad luck. This disappointed him.'

'Fritz covered sheet after sheet of paper with schemes
for discovering new lignite beds and improving the super-
vision of tile-kilns and lime-kilns, with meteorological
records which might help to bring the refinement of
brine to a higher standard, and with notes on the legal
aspect of salt manufacture. But he also saw himself as a
geognost, a natural scientist, who, as he put it, had come
'to an entirely new land, and dark stars'. The mining
industry, it seemed to him, was not a science, but an
art. Could anyone but an artist, a poet, understand the
relationship between the rocks and the constellations?
The mountain ranges, and the foothills with their burden
of precious metals, coal and rock salt, were perhaps no
more than traces of the former paths of stars and planets,
who once trod this earth.

'What has been, must be again,' he wrote. 'At what
point in history will they return to walk among us as
they once did?'

Patiently Karoline Just listened to everything he had learned and therefore needed to repeat to another intelligence. She continued to sew while Fritz ploughed through a *Continuation of the Report on the Purchase of Coal-bearing Plots of Land at Mertendorf*. 'When these data are correlated, one cannot be in any doubt as to the future scheme of acquisition, in the course of which we freely confess that the peasants, by all accounts, will make, in relation to the old prices, fairly high demands . . .'

'Of course they will,' said Karoline, 'but when did you make this report?'

'I did not make it, it was made some time ago. I have to train myself by making reports on reports. That, after all, is what your uncle taught me to do.'

'You have been his best pupil. Indeed, I don't think that he will ever want another one.'

'And yet I don't think that as yet my father takes me seriously.'

'You don't take him seriously,' said Karoline.

'It is my father who must make the application to the administration to consider me for a salaried post. I might hope in the first instance to receive 400 thaler.' She had paused to rethread her needle. 'Justen, how often you must have tried to calculate whether *you* and *he* could keep house on such a sum!'

She realised that his imagination had sped on far ahead of her own, and that the cruel separation between herself and the Unwanted had now become a question of money. The Unwanted, evidently, had no salaried post. This vexed her. Bitterly though she had regretted the whole pretence from its very first moment, it was nevertheless hers. She had created, even if she hadn't meant to, the Unwanted, and she resented his being made into a failure (for he must be more than thirty), and unable to support her as a wife. She felt he had been slighted. She had an impulse to disconcert Hardenberg.

Usually that was easy enough. She told him now — quite truthfully — that although she wished him well, from the bottom of her heart, in his search for a post, she must admit to some doubts about the profession itself. Erasmus was to be a forestry official, well and good, if he ever finished at St Hubertusberg. Karl and Anton were to be soldiers and about that she knew nothing and had nothing to say, but mining, the extraction of minerals and salts from the earth — well, she had been more than once to the salt-refineries at Halle and Artern, and she had seen, and smelled, the clouds of dark yellowish smoke from the amalgam works near Freiberg, and she could not help thinking of them as an offence against Nature, which could never create such ugliness. 'So often, Hardenberg, we have spoken of Nature. Only on Wednesday evening you were saying at table that although human culture and industry may grow, Nature remains the same, and our first duty is to consider what she asks of us.' Taking a risk which she had forbidden herself, she went on, 'You have spoken of Sophie as Nature herself.'

Karoline shut her eyes for a moment as she said this, not being anxious to see the effect. Fritz cried – 'No, Justen, you have not understood. The mining industry is not a violation of Nature's secrets, but a release. You must imagine that in the mines you reach the primal sons of Mother Earth, the age-old life, trapped in the ground beneath your feet. I have seen this process as a meeting with the King of Metals, who waits underground, listening in hope for the first sounds of the pick, while the miner struggles through hardships to bring him up to the light of day. Release, Justen! What must the King of Metals feel when he turns his face to the sunlight for the first time?'

She meant to say, 'I wonder if you have mentioned these ideas to the Direction Committee' – but she could not bring herself to it. She recognised the voice in which he had read to her the opening chapter of *The Blue Flower*. Meanwhile he had opened his file again, and taken out another page of his delicate crocketed writing, another report on a report, this time a summary, in tabular form, of the boiling-points of cooking-salt and salt fertilisers.

41

Sophie at Fourteen

Two days before Sophie's fourteenth birthday, on the 15th of March 1796, the anniversary of his engagement – still not authorised, and indeed not discussed so far, with his father – Fritz went to the jewellers in Tennstedt to have yet another alteration to his ring. It was to contain a tiny likeness of Sophie, he explained, taken from the miniature which had disappointed everybody – that couldn't be helped. Her startled, eager expression was there at least, and her mixture of darkness and brightness. On the reverse, he told them to engrave the words – *Sophie sey mein schuz geist* – Sophie be my guardian spirit. In her birthday poem he wrote:

> *What I looked for, I have found:*
> *What I found, has looked for me.*

In the June of 1796 Fritz wrote to both his father and his mother.

Dear Father,

Not without great unease do I send this letter which I have dreaded for so long. Long ago I would have sent it, if unfavourable circumstances had not arisen. All my hopes depend on your friendliness and sympathy. There is nothing wrong with what lies in my heart, but it is a subject on which parents and children often do not understand each other. I know that you always want to be a patron and friend to your children, but you are a Father, and often fatherly love contradicts the son's inclination.

I have chosen a maiden. She has little wealth, and although she is equal to the nobility, she is not of ancient lineage. She is Fräulein von Kühn. Her parents, of whom the mother is the property owner, lie in Grüningen. I got to know her on an official visit to her stepfather's house. I enjoy the friendship and confidence of the whole family. But Sophie's answering choice long remained doubtful.

Long since would I have sought your confidence and consent, but at the beginning of November Sophie became grievously ill, and even now she is only recovering slowly. You can give back my peace. I beg from you consent and authorisation of my choice.

More by word of mouth. It all depends on you, to make this the happiest period of my life. True, my sphere of activity would be reduced by this match, but I rely for my future on industry, faith and economy, and on Sophie's intelligence and good management. She has not been grandly brought up – she is content with little – I need only what she needs. God bless this important, so anxious, so difficult-to-pass-through hour. It is good to speak out and say what you mean, but you can make me happy only through your consenting Father's voice.

Fritz

Dear little Mother,

I will wait for you at nine in the evening on Wednesday two weeks from now, alone in our garden at Weissenfels. I do not need to ask for anything more, for I know your tender heart.

Fritz

It was true that Hofrat Ebhard had not much idea what to do next, but he was quite used to this. It did strike him that at Schloss Grüningen his patient had too much company, too much excitement, too many little dogs and cage birds, too many visits from the wildly-talking Hardenberg. He sent her for a few days to a rest-home in which he had a part interest, at Weissensee. It was unfortunately damper and much less airy than Schloss Grüningen. 'The house is deserted,' complained Rocken-thien, for George also, just as he was beginning to turn into a decent shot, was to be sent away to school in

Leipzig. There would be only twenty-six people left at home. His worries he shoved to the back of his mind, as one puts a rat-trap on a shelf, when, for the time being at least, it is no longer needed.

'Well, what does he say, the Freiherr?' asked the Mandelsloh.

'I have written to him,' said Fritz, 'and to my mother, and I have explained to them —'

'— what they certainly know already. You have told me that even when your friend from Jena, Assistant Practitioner Dietmahler, came to stay with you, your father questioned him on the subject. It's only Söphgen's name perhaps, that he won't know until he gets your letter.'

'There is something I have to ask you,' said Fritz urgently. 'Let us speak heart to heart. Suppose my father were to refuse his permission. Suppose that he tries to separate me from my Philosophy, my heart's blood. Living here in this paradise you scarcely know what unjust authority means.'

'I know what it is to be separated,' said the Mandelsloh.

'My father himself has been married twice. I am twenty-four years old and there is no law that can be invoked against me in the Electorate of Saxony if I marry without his permission, or indeed against my Sophie, as soon as she reaches her fourteenth birthday. Would she come with me, Friederike, do you think she would defy the world and want no more of it in order to be with me?'

'On what would you support yourself?'

'I would earn the little we need as a soldier, a copying-clerk, a journalist, a night-watchman.'

'These occupations are all forbidden to the nobility.'

'Under another name —'

'— and, I suppose, in another country, if you could get your papers — would you not want to go south?'

'Ah, Frieke, the south, do you know it?'

'Far from it,' said the Mandelsloh, 'who would ever take me there? I shall have to wait until the Regiment is posted to the land where the lemon-trees flower.'

'Well, but you have not answered me.'

'You want her to leave her home, where for as long as she can remember — for God's sake . . .'

'You don't think, then, that she has the courage?'

'Courage when you don't understand what it is that you have to face is no better than ignorance.'

'Treason, Frieke! Courage is more than endurance, it is the power to create your own life in the face of all that man or God can inflict, so that every day and every night is what you imagine it. Courage makes us dreamers, courage makes us poets.'

'But it would not make Söphgen into a competent house-keeper,' said the Mandelsloh. Fritz ignored this and repeated wildly, 'Would she come with me? Could she bear the parting? – my love would make that easy – would she come?'

'God forgive me, I'm afraid she might.'

'Why are you afraid?'

'I forbid you to ask her.'

'You forbid me –'

'– if I don't, another will.'

'But who could that be?'

'Is it possible that you don't know?'

42

The Freifrau in the Garden

THE Freiherr von Hardenberg wrote to Kreisamtmann Just.

> Who was this von Kühn, the actual father of this Sophie? They tell me that he is the son of Wilhelm Kühn, who acquired in 1743, let us say fifty years ago, the proprietorship of Grüningen and Nieder-Topfstedt, and, after that, somehow managed to get a patent of nobility. In good time his son, this Sophie's father, installs himself at Grüningen. His first wife is called Schmidt; she dies. His second wife is called Schaller, then *he* dies. The widow takes up with a certain Captain Rockenthien, I think from the Prince of Schwarzburg's Regiment, thus he in turn becomes the master of Grüningen and Nieder-Topsftedt. I do not think that as yet Rockenthien himself has had the assurance to apply for a patent of nobility.

Kreisamtmann Just replied to Freiherr von Hardenberg.

I can only repeat what I have said before, that I have taught your son all the routine that he needs to know for an official career, and in talking to him I, too, have glimpsed new horizons.

The Freiherr von Hardenberg to Kreisamtmann Just.

Glimpse what horizons you like, but why, in God's name, did you take him to the Rockenthiens?

He took Fritz's letter to Leipzig, where he sat with old friends in the club reserved for nobility, stifling in summer, since the members forbade the waiters to open the steam-clouded windows facing the street. There he consulted old friends, as to how he should answer his eldest son. He button-holed the old Count Julius von Schweinitz and the only slightly younger Graf von Loeben, and asked them what they themselves should do if either of their eldest sons should insist on marrying a grocer's daughter. His mind was, perhaps, beginning to give way a little.

Fritz had asked his mother to meet him in the garden simply so that they would not be overseen by his father, without reflecting what an extraordinary thing it would be for her to do. Auguste nowadays scarcely ever went out at all, never alone, never at night, and certainly never without the Freiherr's considered permission. When she told her maid to get out her black shawl, because she was going out by herself into the garden, the old woman began to say her prayers. Still, by the time the Freifrau had made her way down the unfamiliar back stairs, the alert had been given to everyone in the kitchens and the yard. At the bottom of the steps which led into the upper part of the garden the head gardener was waiting in the dusk with a light to open the gate. That was as well, because she had no key and had given no thought to how she should get in.

In the ordinary way she would have excused or explained herself, but not to-night. She was absorbed not so much in anxiety for Fritz as in gratification at being wanted and needed and told to meet him in the garden.

She stood just inside the gate, listening to the shifting and creaking and strange repeated ticking which birds, in their restless half-sleep, make all night. They lodged in the great cherry tree, which produced two hundred pounds of fruit in a good summer, so that at first light they could start gorging themselves before the gardener's boy arrived. The cherries were almost black, but could still be distinguished from the mass of leaves, gently stirring although there seemed to be no wind.

Fritz was there already, coming towards her up the path from the lower garden. 'Mother, you know I would not keep you waiting.'

The numberless times he had done so no longer

existed. 'Dear Fritz, have you been to see your father?'

'Not yet.'

They sat on two of the old wooden chairs left out all summer under the cherry tree. When Fritz had been born, sickly and stupid, she had been given the blame, and had accepted it. When after months of low fever he had become tall and thin and, as they all said, a genius, she had not been given any credit, and had not expected any. He asked her why she was wearing her winter shawl.

'It's June, mother. Otherwise I should never have asked you to meet me outside.'

Auguste saw now that the shawl was ridiculous. 'But Fritz, I feel safe in it.' He smiled, and did not need to say, 'You are safe with me.'

An extraordinary notion came to the Freifrau Auguste, that she might take advantage of this moment, which in its half-darkness and fragrance seemed to her almost sacred, to talk to her eldest son about herself. All that she had to say could be put quite shortly: she was forty-five, and she did not see how she was going to get through the rest of her life. Abruptly Fritz leaned towards her and said, 'You know that I have only one thing to ask. Has he read my letter?'

Immediately she came to herself. 'Fritz, he surely must have done, but I can't tell. He has never shown me his letters, but then, God forgive me, I did not show him yours. However, the whole household are to join in a prayer meeting tomorrow evening to consider an important family question.'

'But, mother, you are on my side, tell me that is so. You approve of what I have done, and what I am going to do. I am following my heart and my soul, you cannot be against me.'

She cried, 'No! No!' but when he went on, 'In that case, why don't you tell my father what you feel?' she answered, 'But I have to obey him, that is natural.'

'Nonsense, in the world of Nature the female is often stronger than the male, and dominates him.'

'You mean among the birds and insects,' said the Freifrau timidly. 'But, Fritz, they know no better.'

Paying attention only to her mindless tenderness for him, he said, 'You must tell my father that it is not enough for him only to agree to my engagement. We must have somewhere to live, for Sophie and myself to live, the two of us, alone and together. You understand me, you are not too old to have forgotten.'

Auguste allowed herself to remember what she had felt when she and the Freiherr were left, for the first time, alone and together. But what mattered now was her son, almost, for the moment, in the overwhelming summer night, a stranger. 'Indeed, yes, Fritz, of course.'

She could be seen to be struggling with a small package, which she had hidden in the pocket of her top under-petticoat.

'Fritz, my dearest, this is my gold bracelet. Well! I have others, but this is truly mine, it was not given to me by your father, I received it from my godmother when I was twelve, on the occasion of my confirmation. It has been enlarged since then, but only a little, I wish you to have it altered, and made into your engagement rings.'

'The rings have already been made, mother. Look!'

Sophie sey mein schuz geist.

'Indeed, mother, I must not take your bracelet, I do not need it, put it away, consider yourself, or keep it, if anything, for Sidonie.'

Thoughtfulness can be much more painful than neglect. The Freifrau, however, had had very few opportunities to learn this.

Back in her room, which was still at the top of the house, she let herself reflect that if only Fritz could always be at home, even with a new wife, she would want no further earthly happiness. Then she prayed for forgiveness, because she must have forgotten, if only for a moment, the welfare of the Bernhard.

The Bernhard himself, however, thought of it unremittingly. 'What will become of us, Sidonie?' he asked plaintively. 'To whom will you yourself be married? You're difficult, you felt nothing at all for that medical fellow who came on the washday, although he couldn't stop looking at you. You may well be left a spinster.

Karl and Anton, I know, are provided for, and Asmus is supposed to have passed his first exams as a forester . . .'

'I *have* passed them,' said Erasmus. 'The principal congratulated me, so did my father, so did Fritz. He sent me a copy of *Robinson Crusoe*.'

'So, please lend it to me.'

'It's in English,' said Erasmus. 'You can't read English.'

'That is true,' said Bernhard with a deep sigh. 'In those wild forests of words I am lost.'

'In any case,' said Anton, 'you should never lend a book or a woman. There's no obligation to return either.'

'Anton, you are trying to talk like Karl,' said Sidonie. 'But you have not got it quite right.'

'It's simply that I feel the time approaching when a decision will be made about me,' said the Bernhard, standing up among them with the air of the boy Jesus among the Elders in the print on his bedroom wall.

'You know you're to be a page,' said Anton. 'The Electoral Courts of Thuringia and Saxony little know what's coming to them.'

'I appeal to all of you,' the Bernhard cried. 'Who in their senses would think of me as a page? Whatever it is that a page is obliged to do, I know that I could not do it.'

Tears ran down his face, and yet the Hardenbergs were at a kind of ease. Fritz, after he had spoken to his mother, had not stayed even for a night. The Freiherr had departed for a few days, taking with him as a confidential servant the pious Gottfried. Throughout the house there could be sensed, as when music changes not its theme but its key, a little less concentration on the soul, a little more on the body. Today, at half past eight in the morning, they were all still at breakfast. The Freifrau had not come down. Erasmus and Anton sprawled on their chairs. The windows were open down to the ground, the air brought in the scent of the cherry-trees – even of the amarelles, grown for making kirsch, which would not fruit till the autumn – and, from beyond Weissenfels, of the first hay-cutting. All four of them, even the Bernhard, knew that they were not unhappy that morning, but had too much good sense to say anything, even to themselves, about it.

The Freiherr had gone to the Brethren at Neudietendorf to consult the Prediger. At the risk of wordiness, he had spoken of his family properties – bankrupt Oberwiederstadt, the four lost estates, sold to strangers, and Schlöben, the beloved Schlöben-bei-Jena with its poplars and mill-stream, where he hoped to live in his retirement, making it a centre for some of the older Brethren.

'Meanwhile, my eldest son ignores my wishes. If Oberwiederstadt and Schlöben were to be settled upon him, I cannot tell what he would do. It would be only decent for him to marry into the nobility and to find a woman with adequate wealth. Don't tell me I am always thinking about money, it is precisely that I don't want to have to think about it at all. But since the recent events in France the world is turned upside down, and a father's necessities no longer weigh with his sons.'

The Prediger nodded, and said that he would give his advice if Hardenberg would undertake to follow it. The Freiherr gave his word. The next day he rode back to Weissenfels with Gottfried. They stopped at no inns, and exchanged very few words. Silence between them said more.

> *Leipziger Zeitung*, 13 July 1796
> Christiane Wilhelmine Sophie v. Kühn
> Georg Philipp Friedrich v. Hardenberg
> > betrothed
> Grüningen   Weissenfels

43

The Engagement Party

SERVANTS appeared out of the yard gate of the house in the Kloster Gasse. The carrier had brought a pianoforte, ordered by the Freiherr, from Leipzig.

Everyone knows how best to move a piano, or rather, how it should be moved. Not up the front steps, you triple fool! – A little to the right. – It would be easier if we could take off the legs.

When the piano had reached its resting place in the salon and stood unwrapped from its straw and sackcloth, it could be seen to be a thing of beauty, rare in that austere household. Already, however, it had caused trouble enough, since the Father, although he had made up his mind some time ago to replace the harpsichord, had not been able to decide whether to order from Gottlieb Silbermann or Andreas Stein. 'Silbermann's pianos are more sonorous,' wrote the Uncle Wilhelm, 'but the touch is heavier than Stein's. For Stein's, on the other hand, one must send to Vienna.'

'This from Wilhelm,' shouted the Freiherr, 'who

scarcely knows one note from another. The horses in his stable recognise more tunes than Wilhelm.' He continued to take, and discard, advice. 'The French manufacturers are the best,' old Heun assured him. 'They escaped the unpleasant situation in Paris, they have all taken refuge in London, where they live in the British Museum. You may enquire of them there.'

If the Freifrau had been consulted she would have said that she did not care for the pianoforte, as an instrument, at all, and thought it dull in comparison with the sparkling chatter of the harpsichord, which reminded her of her girlhood. The harpsichord, which had now been moved out of the house, was in fact the one she had brought with her to Oberwiederstadt on the occasion of her marriage. It was French, and had a picture of a ruined temple by moonlight on the inside of the lid. But the relentless damp of Weissenfels, where the Saale secretively chose its own time, at any season of the year, to flood its banks, had mouldered it gradually away. The painting had become almost invisible, the jacks were like a row of ageing teeth, some missing. It had come to need re-tuning every evening, and by the morning the pitch was gone. Bits of it, too, appeared to have come unscrewed. 'I dare say I shall be blamed,' said the Bernhard. And in fact Karl complained that they had allowed the Angel to make a *Pfuscherei* of the harpsichord while he was with his regiment. 'But in any case you cannot play it as well as Anton,' said the Bernhard, 'and it is being sold for firewood.'

The Freiherr bought a piano by Johannes Zumpe, one of Silbermann's apprentices, which had been advertised in the *Zeitung*. In this way he succeeded in not following his brother Wilhelm's advice.

Anton was called upon. Anton, who had been thought to have not much interest in life beyond following Karl's example, was now the necessary person. All the family could play – Erasmus could play anything by ear, Sidonie was truly musical, but they could not play like Anton.

The Zumpe piano had a third pedal, which allowed the three lowest octaves to be sustained, while the treble was damped in the ordinary way. Anton sat alone, refusing any help, in the salon. Although it hadn't been one of the Freiherr's requirements when he bought the house, the Hardenbergs' salon had been built originally as a music room and for nothing else, and the airy space faithfully carried every note, balanced it, and let it fall reluctantly.

The Freiherr now told his wife to invite suitable guests from Weissenfels and the surrounding neighbourhood to a *soirée*. 'He is so good-hearted, Sidonie. He cannot rest until he has shared the beauty of the new music.' Hardenberg went out so little, except to meetings of the Brethren and on tours of inspection, that he did not realise that a piano was anything but a novelty at Weissenfels. Chief Magistrate von Lindenau even had a Broadwood, ordered from England to his own specifications.

'Surely what we are sharing is my father's heartfelt pleasure in Fritz's engagement,' said Sidonie.

'Of course, my dear.'

'The party from Grüningen – we can't tell how many will come – cannot, of course, return home the same night. They must all stay here, and you will have to consider about the rooms.'

'How fortunate that we bought the slop-pails!'

No-one in Weissenfels looked forward very much to the Hardenbergs' invitations, but they were so rare – this was not thought of as meanness, everyone knew of their piety and charity – and so formally expressed, that they seemed less of a celebration than a register of slowly passing time, like mortality itself. Most of the guests would be town officials, all would know each other. But none of them would have met the Rockenthiens, except of course the Justs. The Justs had the farthest to come, but would spend the night at the house of old Heun, who was Rahel's uncle.

Lukas was at the door, Gottfried in charge of the *Vorzimmer*, which led into the great downstairs reception room. His last trip with the Freiherr to Neudietendorf seemed to have left him in a position of mild, almost benign authority, which had not been so noticeable before. Erasmus thought it possible that he had been drinking.

'Inconceivable,' said Sidonie. 'You have been too long away from home.'

Small groups of people, in threes and fours, lingered in the Kloster Gasse to watch the Hardenbergs' guests arrive, particularly the rarely-seen country nobility. Old Count Julius von Schweinitz und Krain was driven up in a great barouche like a coffin. 'Take me to some quiet place.' Gottfried gave him an arm to the study.

In the reception room the servants slowly circulated, offering small glasses of arrack. Fritz kept a watch for those whom he thought of as his own friends, and for those who understood poetry – for example, Friedrich Brachmann, the advocate, who had studied with him in Leipzig. Brachmann was crippled from birth, but he walked so carefully, you wouldn't know it (everyone in Weissenfels knew it). Brachmann was hoping to enter the tax department. His limp would not matter there, his ideas about aesthetics would not matter much either. Fritz put an arm through his, and the other one round Frederick Severin.

'Ah, best of friends, I congratulate you,' said Severin. 'And how is the little brother who likes the water?'

'I think he is not supposed to be downstairs,' replied Fritz, 'but I daresay he is.'

Louise, Brachmann's sister, was the dear friend of

Sidonie, who moved towards her as her name was
announced by Gottfried. Louise was twenty-nine, and a
poet.

Both girls were in white, run up by the same dress-
maker, but Sidonie seemed to be moving in flight or in
a drift of whiteness, delicate, weightless, strange to the
onlookers of Weissenfels, while Louise could only hope
not to hear, at least for this summer, the suggestion that
it was perhaps time Fräulein Brachmann should give up
wearing white altogether.

'Oh Louise, Louise, I have spoken to Fritz: he is going
to send your poems to Friedrich Schiller, only you must
keep copies, my dear, because these great men frequently
lose what is sent to them.'

Sidonie's eyes shone with the pleasure of pleasing.
Louise did not reply.

'But that was what you wanted, Lu?'

'Is your brother not going to read them himself?'

Sidonie faltered.

'I am sure he must have done.'

'What did he say to you about them?' Then, after a
moment. 'It does not signify, they are only words, the
broken words of a woman.'

Sidonie wished that the party from Grüningen would
arrive, and fix the attention of the lot of them: then the
piano would surely draw them all together. That the
Rockenthiens had set out she knew, since the Mandelsloh

had had the good sense to send off the stable-boy (the new stable-boy) as messenger the moment they started. The boy, covered with a thick coating of dust, had now arrived, and was being petted in the kitchen. Meantime here were the Justs, Coelestin magnificent in the dark green ceremonial uniform of his rank. Heun, who came with them, was also entitled to a uniform, though not, apparently, one that fitted him. Karoline, who rarely took anything, swallowed half a glass of arrack, and went to stand with Fritz, Erasmus, Severin and Brachmann.

'Where is Sidonie?' she asked.

'With Louise, with poor Louise,' said Erasmus. 'But all that matters is that you have arrived. You are the best friend any of us have, the very best. You are the conciliator. Not even Sidonie can do it so well.'

'That is so,' said Fritz. 'Where Justen is, one can be at peace.'

'Then I hope, *mademoiselle*, you will visit my bookshop,' said Severin.

'Of course she will,' Fritz cried. 'She knows as much about books as I do, and far more about music.'

'There is nothing to know about music,' said Karoline, smiling.

'You must play for us later on.'

'I would not dream of it.'

Fritz bowed and excused himself, having duties everywhere. Karoline looked slowly round her, not allowing herself to watch where he went. She saw the guests as drifts of grey, black, and brown, with the uniforms (since most of those who wore them preferred to talk to each other) as knots of glittering colour, becoming less harsh as the evening light began to fade. The twilight, God be thanked, merciful to us all. The white dresses, now the most conspicuous of all, still lingered on the outer edge of the groups, except for Sidonie's. She had hurried to the side of Senf, who was standing entirely by himself, wearing, to mark his consciousness of his former disgrace (although he had plenty of good clothes), a patched swallow-tail coat. Sidonie was shaking her head at him, and laughing. This seemed extraordinary, for Senf had never been known to say anything amusing. He looked surprised, almost bewitched.

Fritz himself was for the moment with Louise, bending over her awkwardly, but with an instinct of true kindness. The poetess gaped up at him like a fish.

Brachmann drew Erasmus aside a little, towards the windows, and said, 'You know, I have never met Fräulein Just before. She is no longer quite young, but she has worth and serenity.' He paused. 'Do you think she would consider a lame man for a husband?

Erasmus, staggered, was able to answer, 'Oh, but her affections are engaged — I don't know where and I don't know who to, but I do know that much.'

What an embarrassing pair they are, he thought, this

brother and sister. It would be much easier if they could marry each other.

'You were asking about the Bernhard,' said Karoline, left alone with Severin. 'I believe Hardenberg is truly interested in his younger brother. Indeed, he is altogether very fond of children.'

'Quite possibly he is,' said Severin. 'As to Bernhard, you must remember that not all children are child-like.'

44

The Intended

PERHAPS there would never be another evening quite like this in Weissenfels. The guests were waiting, although they were not accustomed to it: even in this great airy room, most of their faces had turned a comfortable fruit-red, but they were unable to settle down to their familiar inspection of each other's costume, followed by discussion, slight advance, slight retreat, circulation, repetition, deep and thick gossip, then indulgence in pickled goose legs, black ham, fruit liqueurs, sweet cakes, more spirits, an amiable progress home, an uncertain climb up to bed. Tonight they could not quite count on anything. Uncertainty and expectancy moved among the guests like the first warning of fever, touching even the most stolid.

Still no Rockenthiens, still no Affianced. In the kitchen, the cook induced the protesting stable-boy, who felt that he was held in some way to blame, to kneel down and pray for his employers' safe arrival.

'They will come,' he blubbered, 'but Fräulein Sophie cannot be hurried, she has been ill.'

The Freiherr was unperturbed, for it had never crossed his mind, since the day when he had agreed to the engagement, to alter any of the arrangements he had made. In fifteen minutes they would all go upstairs to hear the piano, then supper, at which he would not take his place at the head of one of the tables, but would move about, pausing now at one chair, now at another, while Fritz and his Intended sat side by side, then music, and if Sophie's health permitted it, dancing. There were six-and-a-half minutes to go until they adjourned to the music room; he allowed himself a short visit to his old friend Schweinitz und Krain, who was still half-slumbering where Gottfried had left him.

'Hardenberg, what is this I am drinking? Is this what they call punch?'

'Yes, I am told Fritz mixed it up himself.'

'It has to be mixed up?'

'Yes, it seems so.'

'Time wasted, Hardenberg.'

'I will get them to bring you something else.'

'Hardenberg, who are these Rockenthiens?'

The Freiherr shook his head.

'Alas! my old friend!' said the Count.

They had all been swept up the great central staircase, all were seated on faded and tattered chairs brought from all over the house. Most of the candles had been extinguished. Anton, still only fourteen, with raw wrists protruding from his first cadet's uniform, sat down at the Zumpe, where the brightest light fell.

'I will begin with something by Johann Friedrich Reichardt,' he announced boldly. 'I will play one of his revolutionary songs.'

'What is that, boy?' called out the Freiherr.

'Anton, you will start with some religious music,' cried the mother, with the authority of anguish. 'You will play "Wie sie so sanft ruhn".'

Anton turned towards her and nodded. Then the piano lifted its voice, so peaceable, so clear.

The gentle air continued, cut off from any noise in the Kloster Gasse. But then the doors of the music room were thrown open, and light poured in from the broad passage-way outside. Gottfried, although clearly in doubt as to the interruption, introduced Frau von Rockenthien, beautiful but sleepy-looking in a pale violet dress, the Hausherr, a chastened George. But where is She?

'They gave me orders to go ahead,' bellowed Rockenthien. 'My stepdaughter is resting for the moment at the bottom of your stairs.' He advanced on his hosts, huge, weather-beaten, clapping his hands.

'He might be scaring rooks,' muttered Louise Brachmann. 'Heaven help us, they're like a troop of farm-hands come up for the hiring fair.'

The Freiherr received the party with faultless courtesy, making a sign to Gottfried, who set about relighting the candles. Anton, at the end of the next phrase, stopped short, and folded his hands. Where was the Affianced? The elder guests murmured in pity and rank curiosity. She would be carried in, she was debilitated.

But Sophie, quietly followed by the Mandelsloh, came almost running across the room with her old impatience, pale, yes that's true, but eager and high-pitched as ever, transparently ready to enjoy herself. She was dressed in embroidered silk – Chinese silk, they thought – where would that have come from? Her hair was hidden under a white cap, quite appropriate for an Affianced. She wore a single white rose.

'Hardenburch!'

He was there.

'They said I must not come –'

Everyone had thought that this would be the end of young Anton's recital, but the Mandelsloh, who had decided on her tactics as soon as she entered the house, singled out the Freifrau and persuaded her that they must all of them hear it to the very end. The front rows of chairs emptied and shifted to make place for the newcomers. Anton nodded, and continued with a setting of some of Zinzendorf's hymns for the Brethren, passing on to the airs from two or three *Singspiele* and the, what was the piece that he played after that? – that very beautiful piece, I did not know it, could Anton have improvised it himself?

No-one admitted to knowing it, but all half-closed their eyes in pleasure.

He ended with Johann Sebastian Bach's *Capriccio on the Departure of His Brother*. Deeply the audience sighed.

Some of them at least, too, had expected at the supper to see an exchange of rings, after which the father of the future bridegroom, as host, might declare what he intended to give in the way of furniture, feather beds &c. &c., with, perhaps, a list of property. But the Hardenbergs did not do things in that way. The Freiherr only rose to his feet to halt the determined eating and drinking for a few moments, to announce his own happiness and that of his wife's, to welcome them all, and to ask them to join him in a short prayer.

It had also been thought that after the supper, on account of Fräulein Sophie's recent illness, there would be no dancing. But Sophie begged for the musicians.

The Mandelsloh reminded her that Dr Ebhard, perhaps relieved to have something definite to say, had forbidden dancing absolutely.

'I wish I had him here,' cried Sophie. 'I'd make him waltz till his brains boiled.'

She sat between her own mother and Hardenberg's mother, the Freifrau. Frau Rockenthien, as almost always, smiled. She wished Anton was still playing, particularly that piece, rather towards the end, whose name she had been sure she once knew, and she wished she had the baby with her. She was not embarrassed by her husband's loud voice – her first husband had also been very noisy, and neither of them had had any more effect on her than windy weather.

The Freifrau, meanwhile, struggled alone with the demon of timidity. The single glass of arrack which she had taken had not helped her at all. In her heart – although she was afraid this might be a sin of thought – she was terribly disappointed in her future daughter-in-law's appearance. Sophie had a certain touching, bright eagerness but it was a child's brightness. Perhaps because she had never been much to look at herself, Auguste attached great importance to dignity, to height, and to regal beauty. Perhaps Sophie might look better if she let her hair down. Fritz had told her that it was dark.

Since his Intended must not dance, Fritz brought forward the dignitaries of Weissenfels, one by one, to introduce them to her, and among them the younger ones, his own friends. 'I have the happiness to present you to Fraülein von Kühn, who has done me the honour . . . This is Sophie, this is my true Philosophy . . . This is Sophie, this is my spirit's guide in all things . . .'

'O, you must not mind him,' she replied to their congratulations. She was constraining herself not to tap her feet. The music seemed to pass into them and upwards through her whole body: she felt like a bottle of soda-water. A faint rose colour had come at last into her face.

'O, you must not mind him ... when he says such things I laugh.' And she did laugh.

On the whole, Sophie impressed favourably. She was not at all the kind of wife they would have expected for a Hardenberg. But she was artless, and that pleased. Nature always pleases.

How much money would she bring with her? they asked each other.

George, nearly choked by his first high collar and frill, intended to join the dancing as soon as convenient, but did not feel that he had had quite enough to eat to keep his strength up. Downstairs in the half-darkened dining room, which had not yet been cleared, he came across a boy a couple of years younger than himself with the appearance (irritating to George) of an angel. George silently helped himself to cold pigeon-pie, doubling up his left fist in his pocket in case it came to a matter of best man wins, and it was necessary to give the angel a hacking. He said loudly, 'Don't you think my sister Sophie is pretty?'

'You are George von Kühn?' asked the angel.

'That's my business.'

'You are hungry?'

'At home we get more to eat than this ... I asked

you whether you think my sister, who is going to marry your brother Fritz, is pretty?'

'To that I can't give you an answer. I don't know whether she is pretty. I'm not old enough to judge of these things. But I think she is ill.'

George, cramming in more pastry, was disconcerted. 'Oh, there's always someone ill in every house.' The Bernhard said, 'Don't you think my brother Anton played the piano well?'

'The hymns?'

'They were not all hymns.'

'Yes, he played well,' George admitted. 'Where are you going?'

'I'm going out to walk by the river in the darkness. That is the effect the music has had on me.'

George drank off a glass of brandy, as nearly as possible in his stepfather's manner, and staggered upstairs to join the dancing.

The Mandelsloh, against all expectations, was an exquisite dancer, the best, in fact, in the room. But because her husband was not with her, and on account of Sophie, she would not dance that evening, not even with young George, to whom a year or so earlier, she had painfully taught the steps. 'Don't ask me!' she said to Erasmus, when he came trustingly up to her.

'I am not going to ask you to dance, I know I mustn't

aspire to that honour, I am going to ask you to help me.'

'What do you want?'

Erasmus said, 'A lock of Sophie's hair.'

The Mandelsloh slowly turned her head and looked hard at him. 'You too!'

'A very small quantity, to put in my pocket book, close to my heart ... You know, I did not understand her at first, but suddenly it came to me why my brother had the words "Sophie be my spirit's guide" engraved on his ring ...'

She said again: 'You too!'

'A lock of hair, as a souvenir, is surely not so very much, not such a great thing ... I had thought of asking Karoline Just to speak to Sophie, but you, of course, are the right person. Will you have a word with her?'

'No,' said the Mandelsloh. 'If that is what you want, you must ask her yourself.'

Erasmus chose his time carefully. Possibly our times are always chosen for us. The violins in the music room, where the dancing was, struck up a *Schottische*, and he had a curious sensation of not quite understanding what they were, or why they were playing. He seemed to himself to belong to two worlds, of which one was of no possible importance.

Now he was standing next to Sophie's chair, within a

few inches of her delicate body, which smelled a little of sickness. She looked brightly up at him.

'You have hardly spoken to me all evening, Erasmus.'

'I have been making up my mind how to put what I wanted to say.' He stammered it out – of course he was only asking for one curl, one small quantity, not like the *Ringellocke* which Fritz had shown him in the early spring, and which he knew was going to be plaited and set in a locket, or a watch-case. 'A watch-case,' he repeated, 'but of course, not at all like that . . .' Sophie laughed. She had been laughing, it was true, most of the evening, but not with such enjoyment as she did now.

Erasmus, retreating in humiliation, was confronted by the Mandelsloh. 'God in heaven, surely you did not ask her!'

'I don't understand you,' he said. 'You told me – I had thought of you as frank and open . . .'

'Did you expect her to take off her cap?'

He had not thought about it at all.

'Little by little it came away,' the Mandelsloh told him 'on account of the illness. For two months now, quite bald . . .'

She looked at him steadily, without a hint of forgiveness. 'You Hardenbergs shed tears easily,' she said. 'I have had occasion to notice this before.'

'But why did she laugh?' asked poor Erasmus.

45

She Must Go To Jena

FRITZ knew that Sophie was bald, but was confident that her dark hair would return. He knew that Sophie could not die. 'What a man wills himself to do, he can do,' he told Coelestin Just, 'still more can a woman.' But they must not let time slip. Sophie needed better advice, indeed the best. She must go to Jena.

'They are coming to consult Stark. But with whom can they stay?' asked Friedrich Schlegel. 'Hardenberg used to have an aunt here in Jena, but she died, I think about a year ago. The Philosophy, I believe, will be in the charge of her sister, an officer's wife.'

'And Hardenberg's father, *der Alte*, may well, I suppose, be in and out,' said Caroline Schlegel. 'He will be anxious as to our beliefs and our moral life. Woe to the free, woe to the unprayed-over!'

The Jena circle, though not charitable, was hospitable. But the academic year was over, the town was beginning to swelter, the yellow clay soil would soon bake dry, the spire of the Staatskirche seemed to vibrate in the summer's heat. Soon they would all be on vacation, except for poor Ritter, who retreated to his attic and made himself invisible.

Sophie and the Mandelsloh, however, had already moved into lodgings in the Schaufelgasse. The rooms were small, and there were three flights of stairs, but the house was recommended to them because the landlady, Frau Winkler, was used to invalid young ladies. It was clear, indeed, from the first that she had the temperament which is attracted to illness and everything to do with it. This was irritating, but meant that she would bring up jugs of hot water at any time, by night and by day. 'It's part of the attendance, gracious lady,' said Frau Winkler.

At least, the Mandelsloh had thought, reassuring herself, there will be no formality here – not that there was ever much at Grüningen – and poor Sophie can feel as though in her own dolls' house, with the patterned earthenware jugs waiting humbly on the crowded dresser. In truth, though, she was somewhat doubtful about her choice and had to summon up her courage to open her first letter from the Freiherr. She could not know that the Uncle Wilhelm, arriving uninvited at Weissenfels to give his advice, had declared that there were no lodgings in Jena (except perhaps the former palace, where Goethe usually stayed) which were in any way suitable for the Affianced of his eldest nephew.

'The rooms let out by the inhabitants are all at the

top of the house, and are fit only for breeding pigeons. I know the town, better, in all probability, than any of you. This elder sister, take it from me, will have settled for a couple of garrets. Women are always satisfied with too little.'

The Freiherr immediately wrote to Frau Leutnant Mandelsloh that he hoped to come and see her as soon as possible, and that meantime he was entirely assured that she had chosen wisely.

46

Visitors

Friederike's Daybook, July 1796

Söphgen has been trying to keep up her diary, but she must not torment herself any longer to write in it. Let me be the recorder.

We are doing well enough here in our little rooms. Sophie's dinner I prepare myself, rather than sending out to the Rose, in order not to give offence to our landlady. But the Jena air does not suit me, and perhaps it suits no-one, since all the professors and literati seem to have some complaint against each other. Weather very hot. They are beginning to go away on their little outings and vacations. The streets where they live are empty.

Hardenberg's friend Friedrich Schlegel (I think he is not yet a professor) visited us yesterday evening. He too is on the point of some journey or other. I received him by myself. Sophie had gone out with Frau Winkler, to see a military parade. God knows I myself have seen my bellyful of them. But as soon as the pain goes away a little, my beloved little sister is ready to find everything amusing. She is then almost herself.

Well, Friedrich Schlegel. He is a philosopher and a historian. I was not at all put off by his melancholy gaze. He said to me, 'Frau Leutnant, your sister, Fräulein von Kühn, tries to make her mind work in the same way that Hardenberg's does, as one might try to teach a half-tame bird to sing like a human being. She won't succeed, and the ideas she had before, such as they were, are now in disarray and she hardly knows what to put in their place.'

I asked him, 'Have you ever met my sister, Herr Schlegel?'

He replied, 'Not as yet, but I believe she is an instance of a certain easily-recognisable type.'

I said, 'She is my sister.'

Later, Sophie returned in the care of Frau Winkler, who said, with a certain disappointment: 'I expected the young lady to faint, but she did not.'

Although Fritz now had his first official appointment as an Assistant Saline Inspector, and was allowed only short periods of leave, the Rockenthiens left Sophie's treatment entirely in his hands.

'No other system is so reliable as Brown's,' Fritz told Karoline Just, not for the first time. 'To some extent Brownismus is based on Locke's ideas of the nervous system.'

'We have to believe in someone,' said Karoline. 'Another one, I mean, besides ourselves, or life would be a poor thing.'

'I was talking of the exact sciences, Justen.'

Fritz had made a very early start from Tennstedt. There was some delay, however, when he reached Jena, in getting hold of Stark, who was at a professional conference in Dresden. But he was told that it would be possible to see the Professor's Deputy Assistant, Jacob Dietmahler.

'Ah, it's you, what good fortune,' cried Fritz. 'I sometimes think that at every turning point in my life —'

'My life, too, has had its turning-points,' said Dietmahler quietly.

Fritz was overwhelmed. 'Love has made me a monster.'

'Don't concern yourself, Hardenberg. I am happy to have obtained this appointment as a Deputy Assistant, and I have resigned myself to the long walk ahead of me.'

'I am truly sorry if —'

'We won't waste time on that. Why have you come here?'

'Dietmahler, Dr Ebhard will have written the Professor a letter of explanation. My Sophie is in pain.'

'In severe pain, I imagine. I can't, of course, offer any opinion until Professor Stark returns, but Ebhard mentions her complexion, which provides us with an important indication —'

'It is like a rose.'

'This letter says, yellowish.'

But Sophie wanted to go out. She had the remorseless perseverance of the truly pleasure-loving. There had been so little to do in Grüningen. What was more, she had never been serenaded. Here, at least, Dietmahler was able to be of immediate practical assistance. There were plenty of medical students left in Jena, penniless, and working through the vacation in the hope of getting their qualifications a little earlier, or of joining a regiment as a half-qualified bone-setter or wound-doctor. Could they play and sing? Naturally they could. How else can the needy pass their spare time, except with music? Outside the lodgings, in the warm dusk which filled the Schaufelgasse, they began with little airs, little popular songs, then a trio. When the Mandelsloh came down the three flights of stairs, with her purse in her hand, and asked them, 'For whom do you play?' they replied, 'For Philosophy.'

Friederike's Daybook

And now it seems that the great man is actually going to call, that Goethe will actually be among us. We didn't hear this from Hardenberg, but once again from Erasmus, who after all, has not gone to Zillbach, but has a room at the moment at a student's beer-house, where he says he is sleeping on straw. That is emphatically his business, rather than mine. He tells me, also, that it's well known that Goethe cannot endure the wearing of spectacles, and has said, 'What do I gain from a man into whose eyes I cannot look while I am speaking, and the mirror of whose soul is veiled by glasses that dazzle me? A feeling of disharmony comes over me when a stranger approaches me with spectacles on his nose.' I myself used never to wear glasses, but now I do, for fine sewing and for reading, and since we came to Jena I have worn them nearly all the time. On occasion, though, one must ignore great men's fancies.

July 7, morning.
First we tidy our sitting room. With furnishings so poor, there is not much that can be done: they are intended for University assistant-teachers, who are grateful for anything. The medicine bottles, the poultices, the syringes, beloved of Frau Winkler, go into the bedroom; the sewing, the newspapers, under the day-bed. On a day like this, dull and windy, the windows must stay shut, but they do not fit properly. There is a draught, we know that already, but I go closer and confirm it, it is like a skewer. The great man of letters will risk pneumonia, and that must always be held against us.

Söphgen forgets that she is in pain, even that she is ill, in discussing the draught. The secret, says Frau Winkler, is to open the windows now, very wide, just for a time. If the air inside the room is the same temperature as the air outside, no draught can be felt. – But (I tell her) the room will be hellishly uncomfortable. – No matter, cries Söphgen, we'll shut everything tight when he approaches the house, and she collects what is left of her strength and before I can stop her throws the windows wide. Then she begins to cough. 'You should have left that to me. Now your cough pierces me like the nails on the cross. The draught couldn't have done it better.' – And Sophie laughs.

Goethe is coming up the Schaufelgasse. All to the window! He advances in a blue frock coat, and over that a summer dust-coat, a noble garment which almost touches the ground, and does touch the ankles of his splendid boots. He seems to have no servant with him: a private call.

I take off my spectacles and go down, Sophie too, she won't be left behind. She draws herself up, as though she felt no fear. Goethe introduces himself, and taking our hands quite frankly, asks us whether his servant can be accommodated in the kitchen: he *did* bring a man with him after all, but it seems that this man always walks a certain number of paces behind him, imitating, out of respect, his actions and gestures. Surely it would be of much more use if he went in front, and made sure they were going to the right house.

Upstairs, Goethe takes the hardest chair, saying, with much charm, that poets thrive on discomfort. However, in another moment he is pacing up and down the little room.

There is no bell, but I have arranged with Frau Winkler to stamp on one of the loose boards, so that she will know when to bring refreshments. Goethe handily cuts the cake himself, and opens the bottle. He suggests sending down a glass of wine to the servant, which I agree to, although I can't see that he has done much to earn it. Meanwhile he talks a little about health and illness. Some maladies, he says, are nothing but stagnation, which a glass or two of mineral water would remove, but we must never let them linger: we must go straight to the attack, as in all things.

He must see that the case is quite otherwise with our poor little patient. It was clear that he wanted to draw her out. Unfortunately, he does not, as yet, know Hardenberg's poetry, indeed I suppose not much of it, so far, has appeared in print. Sophie, for whom the visit was perhaps too great an honour, could think of nothing to say. At last she ventured that Jena was a larger town than Grüningen. Goethe bowed slightly and replied that Weimar, also, was a larger town than Grüningen.

Sophie did not mention Hardenberg's story *The Blue Flower*. And Goethe, at least, made no reference to the draught.

Erasmus, who had found out exactly when the visit was to be, was waiting, or rather hovering, at the corner of the street.

'Excellency! Please, a word! I am Hardenberg's younger brother – that is, one of his younger brothers. I am a student of forestry – that is, not here . . .'

'I did not think it would be here,' said Goethe. 'There is no school of forestry in the University of Jena.'

'I have been studying at Hubertusberg. That is, I have just left Hubertusberg. May I walk a short distance with you?'

Goethe smiled, and said that there was no law against it.

'You have been calling on Fräulein Sophie von Kühn,' perserved Erasmus, 'and her elder sister, Frau Leutnant Mandelsloh.'

'Ah, she is the elder sister, is she? A woman of strength, I had not quite made out the relationship.' Since Erasmus, coughing, trotting by his side, could manage nothing more at the moment Goethe went on, 'I think I know what you wanted to ask me. You wonder whether Fräulein von

Kühn, when she is restored to health, will be a true source of happiness to your brother. Probably you feel that there is not an equality of understanding between them. But rest assured, it is not her understanding that we love in a young girl. We love her beauty, her innocence, her trust in us, her airs and graces, her God knows what — but we don't love her for her understanding — nor, I am sure, does Hardenberg. He will be happy, at least for a certain number of years, with what she can offer him, and then he may have the incomparable blessing of children, while his poetry —'

Erasmus desperately caught the arm of the great man in mid-speech, spinning him round like flotsam in the tide. 'But that is not what I wanted to ask you!'

Goethe stopped and looked down at him. (The servant, twenty yards behind, stopped also, and stared into a barber's shop.)

'I was mistaken, then. You are not concerned about your brother's happiness?'

'Not about his!' cried Erasmus. 'About hers, about Sophie's, about hers!'

47

How Professor Stark Managed

WHEN Professor Stark returned to Jena he made an examination, and said that an operation was necessary. He would insert tubes, to carry away the poison. There was no other way to drain the gracious Fräulein's tumour. Authorisation was needed from her stepfather in Grüningen. This arrived within twenty-four hours.

'It would be a pity if we were to miss the fireworks for the Elector's birthday,' said Sophie. This was her only objection.

'My stepfather and my mother leave all the details to me,' the Mandelsloh told young Dietmahler, one of whose more awkward duties was to deal with the patients' relatives. 'I shall have to send for my sister's betrothed. He has gone back to Tennstedt. But you, of course, know him well.'

'No, not well, but I have known him for what seems a long time,' said Dietmahler. 'I think his brother Erasmus is in Jena.'

'No, he left yesterday, I advised it. Staying here was

helping neither him nor us. But Hardenberg, of course
– Now, tell me the day and the hour when the Professor
intends to operate. Write them down. Naturally I shan't
forget them, but write them down here in my Daybook.'

But Professor Stark did not manage things in that way.
It was his practice to give as little notice as possible, an
hour at most, of an operation. This was to spare the
patient's nerves. Prevented, too, was the arrival of relatives
long before they were wanted. Dietmahler, of course, had
known this, but was not at liberty to say so. Now he had
to go round once again to the Schaufelgasse with an
explanation.

'The room reserved for the purpose must be kept ready
at all times,' he went on doggedly. 'And there must
be a good supply of old, clean sheets and old, clean
undergarments of the finest linen.'

'Ready at all times, when we don't know when it will
be wanted!' said the Mandelsloh. 'We have two rooms
here, and only two. This is the sitting room, and my
sister is asleep at the moment in the bedroom. You may
leave the inspection to me.'

Dietmahler hesitated. 'And the other things?'

'Do you think we travelled here with piles of old, clean,
cast-off undergarments of the finest linen? Wouldn't we
do better to go back to Grüningen to fetch them?'

'No, the patient must not travel.'

'You mean that your Professor doesn't want to.'

'That is not what I said. How large is the bedroom?'

'The same size as this. One can scarcely move. Tell him he must bring no-one with him, except yourself.'

'Certainly, I can promise that. And your landlady. Would she be ready to be of use?'

'Only too ready.'

'Frau Leutnant, I don't wish us to be antagonists. Could we not look at things another way? I can assure you of the Professor's deepest sympathy and interest. Indeed, he has told me he intends to do the bandaging himself.'

She shook his hand, but it was no more than a truce.

Frau Winkler had discussed the expected visit of Professor Stark with all her neighbours within a certain radius, 'in order that there should be no misunderstanding, when screams and cries are heard. They might imagine some dispute . . .'

'A lodger, perhaps, strangling a landlady,' agreed the Mandelsloh. Frau Winkler, who by now obeyed her slavishly, had been able (since the Great Wash for the year was over) to borrow a quantity of clean old sheets. Strictly speaking, there was no such thing as worn-out sheets in Saxony, but some were thirty or forty years older than others. Holding the material against the broad summer sunshine, she demonstrated how delicately threadbare they were.

'Put them away, speak no more about them, bring me the weekly bill and some coffee,' said the Mandelsloh.

Sophie was out – out for a drive through the cornfields with the wife of the pastor whose sermons they attended on Sundays. They had started early, to avoid the sun, and had driven through roads shadowed with poplars.

'Thank you, Frau Pastor, you have been so very kind, you are so kind, you will be so kind I am sure as to excuse me for being tired so quickly.'

'I may perhaps be allowed to call for Fräulein Sophie next week?' said the pastor's wife, but the Mandelsloh intervened politely, saying that unfortunately they could not be sure of their arrangements.

'I wish George was here,' said Sophie.

'George!'

'I don't know why, we were not speaking of him, but I wish he was here.'

Hardenberg so far knew nothing about the operation. Possibly he did not even know that they were still in Jena. He himself, the Mandelsloh believed, was inspecting the Salines at Dürrenberg. But the Professor's instructions, which, in spite of her critical attitude, she took in a spirit of military obedience, were still, 'I will give you an hour's notice. That is best. Afterwards you may summon anyone you wish.'

It was Dietmahler, again, who brought this last message, and Dietmahler who appeared, bringing with him a hospital servant, on the morning of the 11th of July.

'The operation will take place at eleven o'clock. I will explain what has to be done.' The double bed was dragged to the middle of the room and made up with the ancient sheets, the front room sofa was piled with bandages, lint and sponges which the hospital servant had brought with him. Sophie seemed not to be disturbed.

Frau Winkler announced that a man was at the door. He was a messenger, with a note to say that the Professor found that he must postpone the operation until two in the afternoon.

'Just to remind us that he is a great man,' said the Mandelsloh.

'Frau Leutnant, that is unjust,' said Dietmahler.

He sent the hospital servant to an eating house, and walked the streets of Jena until a quarter to two. When he returned, Sophie was wearing an old wrapper, frail and yellowish, almost the same tone as her skin. She appeared smaller, perhaps shrunken. The Mandelsloh thought, 'What am I doing with what was entrusted to me?'

Two carriages, closed in spite of the high summer's day, turned into the Schaufelgasse. They drew up, the doors opened. 'There are four of you,' said the Mandelsloh, turning in bitter reproach on Dietmahler. 'You gave me your word . . .'

'Three of them are pupils,' said Dietmahler miserably. 'They are learning how these things are done.'

'I, too, am learning how these things are done,' said the Mandelsloh.

From the bottom of the stairs someone could be heard dismissing, or at least restraining, Frau Winkler. The Professor and his students made their appearance, correctly dressed in black. The students' frock-coats were absurdly too large. Doubtless they had been borrowed. The Professor bowed to the ladies. Sophie smiled faintly.

'We will administer the cordial.'

It was a mixture of wine and laudanum, to Dr Brown's prescription, which Sophie drank down without protest. Then to the bedroom, where all must skirt awkwardly round the bed in its unaccustomed place. The students, to be out of the way, stood with their backs to the wall, darting sharp looks, like young crows, each taking out the pen and inkwell from behind his lapel.

Sophie was helped onto the pile of borrowed mattresses. Then the Professor asked her, in tones of grave politeness – suitable, in fact, to a child on its dignity – whether she would like to cover her face with a piece of fine muslin. 'In that way you will be able to see something of what I do, but not too clearly ... There now, you cannot see me now, can you?'

'I can see something glittering,' she said. Perhaps it was a game, after all. The students wrote a line in their notebooks.

Following the medical etiquette of Jena, the Professor motioned Dietmahler to his side, and asked him,

'Esteemed colleague, am I to make the incision? Is that what you advise?'

'Yes, Herr Professor, I advise it.'

'You would make two incisions, or one only?'

'Two, Herr Professor.'

'So?'

'So.'

Frau Winkler, waiting below on the bottom stair, had been able to hear nothing, but now her patience was rewarded.

48

To Schlöben

BETWEEN Artern and Jena, Langensalza and Jena, Dürrenberg and Jena, Fritz traversed the dusty summer roads,
crowded now with migrants and soldiers. In his notebook
he wrote —

> I am like a gambler who has risked everything on one
> stake.
> The wound I must not see.

Sophie underwent another operation to drain the
abscess on the 8th of August, 1796. A third, towards the
end of August, was necessary because the other two had
been completely unsuccessful. Professor Stark spoke of
things going as well as could be expected. The patient's
forces were not declining, the pus was only moderate.
The autumn, however, was always a dangerous time,
particularly for young people.

Sophie to Fritz: 'Hardly, dear Hardenberg, can I write
you a line but do me the kindness not to distress yourself
— This asks heartily your Sophie.'

*　　*　　*

On each of the two fathers the third operation had profound effects. Rockenthien's noisiness, his persistent looking on the bright side, his dirty jokes, all vanished, not gradually but overnight, as though a giant hand had closed over him, squeezing him clear of hope. The Freiherr, on the other hand, for the first time in his life, wavered – not in his religious faith, but on the question of what to do next. Until the end of August, he put off visiting Jena. Then he made up his mind to go, taking as many as possible of his family with him, and staying the night at Schlöben-bei-Jena. Even this was partly an attempt to get rid of the Uncle Wilhelm, who was still a guest at Weissenfels. 'I shall remain here, brother, until I can see that my advice is no longer needed.'

'Very good,' said the Freiherr, 'then you will not be coming to Schlöben.' He gave orders for only six or seven bedrooms to be prepared.

For themselves and a week's provisions they would need both the carriages, and four of the long-suffering horses. Fritz was already in Jena, Anton was at military school in Schulpforta, but Karl was at home – half the officers in his regiment had been on leave since Saxony had withdrawn from the coalition against the French – and Sidonie, and Erasmus. The Bernhard had not much wanted to come, but neither did he want to be left at Weissenfels with the baby, the servants and his Uncle.

* * *

The Freifrau, jolting along beside Erasmus, knew that it could not be right, in the middle of the distress she felt for Sophie, to recognise even a moment's happiness, and yet her heart beat faster when they turned into the familiar valley and for the first time in three years it was time to look out for the four great chimney-stacks of Schlöben, and the tops of the poplars. She had always loved the place. Perhaps because the house was thickly surrounded with trees, it gave her an unfamiliar feeling of safety. Anton had been born here, and a little girl, Benigna, who had not survived. Her husband, she knew, even though they came here nowadays so rarely, said on no account would he ever part from Schlöben.

'The chimneys!' cried Sidonie, who was sitting up by the driver.

They passed the oak tree with the ropes of their old swings still hanging from a high branch and a lower one. To the right was the humpbacked bridge which crossed both the stream and the footpath and led to the farm buildings and the chapel.

The property was dark and damp, and in such bad repair that the top flight of the main staircase was no longer safe and the servants had to reach their bedrooms by way of ladders. The *Gutsverwalter*, too, had moved into the great house, simply for the sake of shelter, since his own place was in ruins. But there was none of the digni-fied wretchedness of Oberwiederstadt, rather a diffused sense, in that misty valley, of relaxation, of perpetual forgiveness, of coming home after having done one's best.

Karl, sentimental like all military men, had tears in his eyes as they passed the remains of the swings, the old sledge-run down from the top of the valley, the pond, dry now until the autumn. He thought too of the months he had spent here not long ago, after his plans to marry money had ended in confusion, and he had had to take refuge from a furious and insulted woman.

'We used to put straw in our boots in winter,' said Sidonie.

'And take them off before we went indoors,' said Karl. 'How white your feet used to look, Sido, just like a fish, not like ours at all. Should you like to be a child again?'

'I should prefer us all to be children,' said Erasmus, 'then we should have a kingdom of our own.'

'That is not at all my experience,' said the Bernhard.

When he was very young the Bernhard had believed that the six-year gap between himself and Sidonie would gradually disappear and that just as he would come to be as tall as she was, or taller, so he would grow to be the same age as she was, or older. He had been disillusioned.

The warm twilight smelled of linden trees and chicken dung. 'Listen to the stream,' said Sidonie. 'We shall be able to hear it muttering away all night.'

The Bernhard replied that he preferred to live by a river.

While the luggage was being slowly unshipped, the house doors opened and the *Gutsverwalter*, Billerbeck, came out, followed by some flustered poultry, who evidently also considered the house as home. Everyone lived at the back. The front entrance was scarcely used. Through the pearly dusk which filled the main hall you could see the distant lighted kitchen at the end of a cavernous passageway.

Between the Freiherr and his *Gutsverwalter* there was scarcely any formality. Almost the same height as each other, they embraced warmly.

'We have suffered, we are suffering, Billerbeck. God is testing us.'

'I know it, Excellency.'

Four years ago, when he was last in Schlöben, Bernhard had been quite a small boy, sharing a four-poster with one of his brothers — he was almost sure it had been Erasmus — in a large room on the first floor. This room like most of the others on the north side had been seriously damaged since then by rain driving in through the broken windows. Any day now, Billerbeck repeated again and again, the repairs will be put in hand. Meanwhile, the Bernhard was lodged in a slip of a room on the second floor in a bed not much larger than a cot.

'My father and mother are already in bed and asleep,' said the Bernhard to himself. 'There is no wind, but from time to time the moon shines in and the room becomes bright. Somewhere, too, a clock is ticking.' And so it was, even though he could not see it. High up on the outer south side of Schlöben was an enormous and ancient gilded clock-face which set the time, even if not quite accurately, for the whole household; its works were in the thickness of the wall of the room where the Bernhard lay. 'I am lying restlessly in my bed,' he went on. 'Everyone else has heard what I did, and yet none of them give it serious attention.'

For some time now it had come to him that the opening chapter of Fritz's story was not difficult to understand. It had never been shown to him, or read to him. But there was nothing of any interest to him at Weissenfels that he had not had a good look at.

He had been struck – before he crammed the story back into Fritz's book-bag – by one thing in particular: the stranger who had spoken at the dinner table about the Blue Flower had been understood by one person and one only. This person must have been singled out as distinct from all the rest of his family. It was a matter of recognising your own fate and greeting it as familiar when it came.

49

At the Rose

THEY started for Jena next morning at five o'clock. The barely drinkable first coffee was served to them in the morning room. Outside, at the head of the valley, the sky was barred with long streaks of cloud which seemed to be waiting for the dawn to burn them into transparency. Schlöben itself, except for the glitter of the stream, was in shadow. 'You can hardly imagine the strange mood I'm in,' said Karl. 'I should like to sit at this window until the whole place grows bright.' 'We are enchanted here,' said Sidonie. 'Until we get started, we shan't be able to realise the depth of our unhappiness. We have come to see poor Fritz, and yet we're farther away from him than ever. I'm ashamed to feel such peace.'

'*Satt!*' cried Erasmus, banging down his coffee cup.

With an early start, they could return to Schlöben that evening, giving the horses eight hours' rest. At Jena, the Freiherr had reserved a large private room for them at the Rose. In spite of the family's difficulties he always went to the best inns, for he knew of no others.

'There is Fritz!' shouted Karl, who was driving the first carriage and turned well in front of the others into the yard of the Rose.

'No, that is not my brother!' cried Sidonie. First out, jumping down without waiting for the step to be fixed, she ran towards him. 'Fritzchen, I hardly knew your face.'

Such a large party, of course, could not arrive all at once at Frau Winkler's. The Freiherr would call there first, the others later.

'Should I not accompany you, Heinrich?' asked the Freifrau, summoning up all her reserve of courage. No, he would walk there with Fritz. They would start at once. The rest went into the Rose and upstairs to the handsome front room overlooking the square.

'There they go,' said Karl, lifting one of the white linen blinds. 'When did we last see the two of them walking together like that?'

After Fritz and the father were out of sight a group of prisoners, fettered by the leg, came to clean the street. Whenever the guard lost interest in them they laid down their brushes and held out their hands for charity. Sidonie threw out her purse.

'They will cut each others' throats for it,' said Karl.

'No, I am sure they have a system of distribution,' said Erasmus.

'Very probably the youngest will get least,' said the Bernhard.

'Coffee, coffee, for the respected ladies and gentlemen!' called the landlord, who had followed them up. A waiter in a striped apron asked if they desired wine.

'Not yet,' Erasmus told him.

'I want you to lie down,' said Sidonie to her mother. 'These sofas seem expressly designed not to be lain upon, but all the same, I want you to try.'

The Freifrau lay down. 'Poor Fritz, poor sick Söphgen. But it will cheer her to see our Angel.' She motioned to the Bernhard to come and sit beside her. The room was already growing warmer. The broad blinds hung without the slightest tremor.

The next arrival was Dietmahler, sent by Professor Stark to see if he could be of assistance. He hesitated in the doorway, looking from face to face in the shadowed room. He had come into the Rose and upstairs without being announced. They were all talking to each other, no-one looked round, and Dietmahler unwisely confided in the blond child who was standing close to him, examining the hydraulics of the coffee-urn.

'You are Bernhard, aren't you? I am a friend of your brother Friedrich, I have been to your house in Weissenfels. I don't know whether your sister Sidonie remembers me.'

'Very likely not,' said the Bernhard. 'However, I remember you.'

Sidonie, half hearing, came towards them, smiling. Naturally she remembered everything – the washday, the happiness of his visit, and, of course, he was –

'Of course,' said the Bernhard.

'I have now the honour to be the Deputy Assistant to Professor Stark,' said Dietmahler. 'You may have heard your brother mention me in his letters, in connection with the treatment of his Intended.' He took out his professional card.

That would bring his name to her mind, no doubt of it. But the few moments during which she had not been able to remember it confirmed Dietmahler in what, after all, he already knew, that he was nothing. What means something to us, that we can name. Sink, he told his hopes, with a kind of satisfaction, sink like a corpse dropped into the river. I am rejected, not for being unwelcome, not even for being ridiculous, but for being nothing.

'Dietmahler!' Erasmus called out. Now Sidonie did remember, and covered her face for a moment with her hands. 'Dietmahler, thank God you are here, you will tell us exactly what is happening. You haven't been practising long enough to know how to tell lies.'

'That is not very polite,' said Karl.

'Fräulein von Kühn is still feverish,' said Dietmahler. 'Long visits are out of the question; half an hour, perhaps. Unfortunately, her cough delays the healing of the incision. It splits open. The Professor believes now that if he was given permission to carry out one further operation we might hope for an immediate and complete recovery.'

'And what do you believe?' asked Erasmus.

'I don't question the Professor's prognosis.'

After this, Dietmahler excused himself. He had to think, he said, of his other duties.

'Of course you must,' cried Sidonie. 'And you must forgive us, but we are anxious. Even now we can't truly believe that you have any other patient but Fritz's Söphgen. People in distress are selfish beyond belief.'

'That is what your brother said to me.'

'Then he showed more sense than usual.'

She was trying to make amends, although she did not know what for. Then he was gone, and having nothing else to do, they stood at the window and watched him, in his turn, crossing the cobbled street to walk in the shade.

The Freifrau was sleeping uneasily. The landlord again asked if he should send up a few bottles of wine.

'If it will make you happy, yes,' said Karl.

'Wine from the district, Herr Leutnant?'

'Heaven forbid, bring Moselwein.'

As soon as the waiter had come and gone, Erasmus broke out violently. 'Father will soon be back, since he is allowed to visit for only half an hour. We have managed very badly. What will come of his visit? You know that whatever consent or permission he has given, he still considers the marriage quite unsuitable—'

'It is quite unsuitable,' the Bernhard interrupted him. 'It is our business to see the beauty of that.'

'You should not have come here, Angel in the House,' said Erasmus angrily.

'Nor, I think, should you,' said the Bernhard.

Turning to Karl, Erasmus went on, 'Why has the father been permitted to call so soon upon Söphgen, whose condition, poor soul, has had such an effect on Fritz that his own sister did not recognise him? What must he feel now? As a parent and a Christian he must pity her, but beyond that he can only think that his eldest son is to be tied for life to a sick girl, who may never be able to bear him children. He will have to withdraw his consent. No-one could expect him to do otherwise. And then it will be a matter for poor Fritz, the wretched Fritz, to break the cruel truth — to say: my dearest Philosophy, I regret that my father does not think you fit to share my bed —'

'My mother is waking up,' said Sidonie.

On the stairs there sounded a heavy tread which sent a tremor through the new sash-windows of the best room at the Rose. The Freiherr stood before them, with tears running down his face — to that they were accustomed at prayer-meeting, the tears of true repentance — but he was sobbing with grotesque intakes of air, with hiccoughs, as though choking over a gross mouthful.

'The poor child ... ough! ... the poor child ... so ill ... ough! ... and she has nothing ...'

He leaned − something none of them had ever seen before − against the frame of the door, grasping it with both hands.

'I shall give her Schlöben!'

50

A Dream

KARL pointed out that the father had no power to do anything of the kind. He had inherited Schlöben from his uncle, Friedrich August, in 1768, and it was entailed on Fritz, born four years later. But that did not take away in the least from the generosity of the sacrifice, inspired purely by human compassion, which the Freiherr had wished to make. — The Bernhard thought that it did take away from it a little.

At this time Fritz had a persistent image which hovered at the edge of his dreaming mind. Finally he stood aside to let it in. He was a student once again in Jena, listening to Fichte's lecture on the Self, and it came to him that he should not be doing this, that he was in the wrong place, because he had heard that his friend Hardenberg lived only two hours' ride away, at Schlöben. His horse was not a good one, and he did not arrive until it was dark. He knocked at the door, which was opened by a young girl with dark hair. He thought that this might be his friend Hardenberg's wife, but did not like to ask.

At Schlöben he lived as a welcome guest for two weeks. When the time came for him to leave, his host accepted his thanks, but told him he must not come again.

Fritz wrote down the incident as it had come to him, one paragraph only. Since he had to go to Tennstedt, he asked Karoline Just whether he might read it to her.

'This is like past times,' he said, looking round, as though surprised, 'the parlour, the firelight, your uncle and aunt gone to bed, the reading.' Karoline thought, 'He never used to talk in this way. He might be one of the neighbours.' Fritz opened his notebook.

'I must tell you that this is the story of a dream.'

'In that case I can only listen to it on account of our long friendship,' said Karoline. 'You must know that people are only interested in their own dreams.'

'But I have dreamed it more than once.'

'Worse and worse.'

'Justen, you mustn't speak carelessly of dreams,' he told her. 'They are responsible for things such as have not appeared for seven years in philosophy's house of fools.'

While he read aloud she thought, 'Seven years ago I did not know him.'

'Is it worth going on with, Justen?'

'Let me read it through once to myself.' Then she asked, 'What did the young woman look like?'

'That doesn't matter. What matters is that she opened the door.'

The Freiherr's old friends and his colleagues at the Salines, even Coelestin Just, spoke of his gesture — the gift of Schlöben to Sophie von Kühn — as an absurd example of *Herrnhuterei*. About the legal position none of them were quite sure, but 'it is unheard of, uncalled for,' said old Heun. 'Our Lord himself did not do so much. Hardenberg's sons out-at-elbow, the Oberwiederstadt estate penniless, this is not the time for excessive loving and giving.' Senf pointed out sharply that the Schlöben estate was also penniless.

These things, of course, were not said in the presence of Kreisamtmann Just, but he was well aware of them. Even in his garden-house melancholy caught him by the sleeve. 'It is only that you have been spoiled,' said Karoline. 'You have myself and Rahel, who are fixed in our ways, so that it's hard to imagine that we could ever change. And when your old friend behaves in a certain way, so that he seems quite a different person, you feel that old age itself is approaching "with silent step".'

'The truth is,' her uncle told her, 'the truth is, that old Hardenberg has not changed. Give and take, he has always been impossible to understand. I call this Hardenbergianismus. But one must not complain, when a man is listening to messages from God.' He looked more

closely at his niece, and said, 'It is absurd for you, Karolinchen, to call yourself fixed in your ways.'

'But, fixed or not, I am always welcome here,' said
Karoline, smiling, 'you always tell me that, are you not
going to say it this time?'

'Tell me what I am to think, Erasmus, Karl, Sidonie,' the
Freifrau asked. 'I do not quite understand what has been
proposed. Does Schlöben no longer belong to us?'

'Put your mind at rest,' Erasmus told her. 'Our poor
Sophie is interested only in going back to Grüningen.'

The Freifrau felt relief and at the same time a certain
resentment, which only the Bernhard noticed, at what
seemed almost a criticism of Schlöben. Was it possible
that the girl did not want to live there? 'But if your
father wishes it,' she said, 'she must be made to.'

51

Autumn 1796

By September carts were beginning to make their way into Jena from the pine-woods with logs for the coming winter. Branches from the tops of their loads scraped against the windows in the side-streets, which were littered with twigs like a rookery. Manholes opened suddenly in the pavements, and gratefully received the thundering rush of wood. At the same time, pickling had begun, and enormous barrels of vinegar began to trundle down the rungs into the reeking darkness of the cellars. Each house stood prepared according to its capacity, secreting its treasure of vinegar and firewood. The students were back, 'and the whores,' said the Mandelsloh. 'They have been trying their luck somewhere else during the vacation, Leipzig or Berlin.' They came back to Jena in modest wagonettes, though not to the streets near the Schaufelgasse. This was a disappointment to Sophie, who would have liked to have a sight of them. The *Fakultät*, also, returned to their houses and issued their announcements for the coming winter months. There were the free public lectures, many more private ones and some *privatissime*, the most expensive of all. Professor Stark was lecturing, *privatissime*, on female disorders.

Fritz, while he was still at Tennstedt, received a letter from the Schaufelgasse in a writing he did not know. From the signature he saw that it was from Leutnant Wilhelm Mandelsloh, the man himself, on leave from the Regiment of Prince Clemens zu Langensalza. His letter was undertaken, he said, at the command of his wife. Sophie herself could not sit comfortably for long at a writing table, and his wife made the excuse that she was busy with women's matters ('They want to give him something to do,' Fritz thought) so they had left it to him to give an account of the patient's health. – In spite of what he had said, Sophie managed to include a note, saying that she was very well, only unfortunately she was sometimes rather ill, and sending a thousand kisses.

At the end of November the Leutnant's leave was up, and he had to return, perhaps with some relief, to Langensalza. He may well have concluded that he was no longer of much importance to his wife's scheme of things.

The Schlegels and their hangers-on did not call at the Schaufelgasse, relying on Dietmahler to keep them posted. He could only say that Sophie's fever came and went, while the incision repeatedly healed up on the outside, then broke out once again and discharged on the inside. Stark prescribed an increased dose of laudanum, which Dietmahler brought round twice a week.

'I wish you good fortune in your future career,' said the Mandelsloh. They would be back in Grüningen by Christmas, and for Sophie's birthday, in March.

'Yes, she will be fifteen in the spring,' Dietmahler told Caroline Schlegel. 'Everything is still to be hoped for, both in mind and body.'

'That I can't see,' replied Caroline. 'Hardenberg can only hope that she will get older, which, it seems, she may well fail to do.'

Dietmahler thought to himself, 'There is no reason why I should stay in Jena, or with these people, or indeed in this country. All I need is a word from someone of importance to recommend me. I might perhaps go to England.' Although Dr Brown was dead, two of his sons, Dietmahler believed, were practising in London. 'As to my mother, I could see to it that she received money regularly, or she could come with me.'

52

Erasmus is of Service

'FRITZ, best of brothers,' said Erasmus. 'Let me be of service to you. Until it's decided where my first appointment is to be, I am nothing but an encumberer of the ground. Let me escort your Sophie and the Mandelsloh back to Grüningen.'

It had to be soon, before the winter roads made the journey impossible for an invalid. Already, the Mandelsloh had thought of almost everything necessary. She had hired a closed carriage and seen to it that the horses were roughshod, in case of freezing weather, she had sent the heavy luggage on ahead, called on the wife of Professor Stark and presented her with a farewell present of silver-gilt asparagus knives, given the servants their tips, written a restrained note to the Schlegels and allowed Frau Winkler to weep for half an hour on her shoulder. All that Erasmus had to do was to ride alongside the carriage, a round-faced, unimpressive escort, and to be on duty at each stop. When they got within ten miles of Grüningen, he must press on ahead, to give notice of their arrival. This would be of some, if not very much, use to Sophie. His real motive was one of the strongest known to humanity, the need to torment himself.

The first day they started late, and covered only ten miles. At the Bear at Mellingen Sophie was taken straight up to her room. 'Already she is asleep,' said the Mandelsloh when Erasmus came into the inn parlour from seeing to the baggage. She had engaged the inn-keeper's niece to wait in Sophie's room and call her immediately if she was needed.

At rest for once, she was sitting, between the uneven light and shadow of the candles and the glowing stove above which, in a great arched recess, boots were propped up to dry and dishes were kept warm. The radiance fell across the left side of her serviceable face and turned it into gold, so that to Erasmus for the moment she looked not quite the Mandelsloh.

'The *Abendessen* is ready,' she said. He thought, she is a warrior saint, a strong angel of the battlefield.

'I have been to the kitchen,' she went on. 'Stewed pigs' trotters, plum conserve, bread soup.'

'I cannot eat,' said Erasmus.

'Come, we're Saxons. We can make a good dinner, even if our hearts are breaking.'

Erasmus sighed. 'So far, at least, the journey has not made her any worse.'

'No, not any worse.'

'But the pain —'

'I would bear it for her if I could,' said the Mandelsloh. 'People say that and hardly mean it. I, however, do mean it. But time given to wishing for what can't be is not only spent, but wasted, and for all that we waste we shall be accountable.'

'The years have taught you philosophy.'

To his amazement she smiled and said, 'How old do you think I am?'

He floundered. 'I don't know . . . I have never thought about it.'

'I am twenty-two.'

'But so am I,' he said in dismay.

53

A Visit to Magister Kegel

HAUSHERR von Rockenthien had not exactly been much loved in Grüningen, but his laugh was missed. Being a man without guile, he continued in the same manner as always, holding out his great arms, embracing his friends, whistling up the dogs to go shooting, but now, as though some mechanism had broken, without laughing.

It was not odd that he should go down into the town to see Magister Kegel. That had always been his way, he was too impatient to summon anyone up to the Schloss and wait until they arrived. What was unusual was that his wife should go with him. Even at this time of anxiety she remained as inactive or, to use a kinder word, as tranquil as ever. Still, the trap was brought round to the frosty front drive and both got in, the springs, on the Hausherr's side, rocking violently, as he took his seat.

'The weather was just like this,' he said, 'when Coelestin Just first brought Hardenberg to our house.'

'I rather think it was snowing,' said Frau Rockenthien.

Magister Kegel, since his retirement, had lived with his

books in a small house near the subscription library. He congratulated Rockenthien on the return of his step-daughters from Jena. Everyone in the district had missed Fräulein Sophie. He hoped most earnestly that, God willing, her health was on the mend, but he was not at all anxious to come up to Schloss Grüningen.

'All the teaching you have required me to do at your house I have done. I have nothing to reproach myself with, but the results have been uniformly discouraging. Your two youngest have not, so far, been entrusted to me – but, in my view, poor Fräulein Sophie should on no account attempt to study, while she is ill, what was too difficult for her when she was well. I consider it quite inappropriate. It would be a pantomime.'

'It is what she wishes, however,' said Rockenthien.

'To what did she think of applying herself?'

'I think she would like to learn something rather showy,' said Rockenthien eagerly, 'or I had better say noteworthy, to astound her betrothed.'

'I am not the person from whom to acquire anything showy,' said the Magister, looking round at his modest possessions. 'And perhaps I may take the opportunity to say, that I think von Hardenberg has always been far too much indulged in your house.'

'All the young people in my house are indulged,' said Rockenthien miserably. He saw that Kegel was on the verge of refusing absolutely to come. Frau Rockenthien, who had so far said nothing, in fact said nothing now. It was possible that she was scarcely thinking at all. Kegel, however, looked intently at her as she rose from her chair, nodded slightly, and said that unless he heard to the contrary he would call at the Schloss the following Wednesday, 'but I should not wish to interrupt any medical treatment.'

'You need not fear that,' Rockenthien told him, 'Söphgen is now in the charge of Langermann, who prescribes for her nothing but goat's milk.'

Dr Langermann, who had taken over from Dr Ebhard, was a cosy, old-fashioned practitioner who was known to every family of good standing in Grüningen. It was his private opinion that they had been poisoning Fräulein Sophie in Jena. Recovery would come in the spring, when the goat's milk would be at its best.

54

Algebra, Like Laudanum, Deadens Pain

AT Weissenfels they talked about the Neutrality Conference which had very nearly been held in the town but in the end, to the dismay of the tradespeople, hadn't been, about the Prussian disasters, about the death of the old whore of Babylon in St Petersburg, and about Hardenberg's Intended. But Fritz himself no longer saw his old friends, not the Brachmanns, not even Frederick Severin. 'You cannot expect him to be good company,' Sidonie told them. 'As soon as he has finished his office work for the day he goes up to his room. You can knock, and knock, but he doesn't answer. He has withdrawn to the kingdom of the mind.' Severin replied that the mind had many kingdoms. 'Fritz is studying algebra,' said Sidonie.

'Algebra, like laudanum, deadens pain,' Fritz wrote. 'But the study of algebra has confirmed for me that philosophy and mathematics, like mathematics and music, speak the same language. That, of course, is not enough. I shall see my way in time. Patience, the key will turn.

'We think we know the laws that govern our existence. We get glimpses, perhaps only once or twice in a lifetime, of a totally different system at work behind them. One day when I was reading between Rippach and Lützen, I felt the certainty of immortality, like the touch of a hand. – When I first went to the Justs' house in Tennstedt, the house seemed radiant to me, even the green tablecloth, yes, even the bowl of sugar. – When I first met Sophie, a quarter of an hour decided me. – Rahel reproved me, Erasmus reproached me, but they were wrong, both of them wrong. – In the churchyard at Weissenfels I saw a boy, not quite grown into a man, standing with his head bowed in meditation on a green space not yet dug up, a consoling sight in the half darkness. These were the truly important moments of my life, even though it ends tomorrow.

'As things are, we are the enemies of the world, and foreigners to this earth. Our grasp of it is a process of estrangement. Through estrangement itself I earn my living from day to day. I say, this is animate, but that is inanimate. I am a Salt Inspector, that is rock salt. I go further than this, much further, and say this is waking, that is a dream, this belongs to the body, that to the spirit, this belongs to space and distance, that to time and duration. But space spills over into time, as the body into the soul, so that the one cannot be measured without the other. I want to exert myself to find a different kind of measurement.

'I love Sophie more because she is ill. Illness, helplessness, is in itself a claim on love. We could not feel love for God Himself if he did not need our help. – But those who are well, and have to stand by and do nothing, also need help, perhaps even more than the sick.'

55

Magister Kegel's Lesson

SOPHIE'S bedroom was crowded: the air was thick as wine. Noisy, too, with the little ones competing on their highest pitch, George's voice imitating someone — it was the voice he used for imitations — the shrieking and rattling of the cage-birds, witless barking.

'I cannot conduct a class among such disorder,' exclaimed the Magister, as a servant showed him in. 'Kindly remove the five dogs, at least, from the room. Where is Frau Leutnant Mandelsloh?'

'My stepfather begged her to come down and put things straight in his office,' said George.

'Ah, George. I have not seen you for some time.'

Sophie was lying among shawls on a little day-bed.

'Ach, dear Magister, George was giving — he was giving a little —'

'He was giving an impersonation of myself. That I could make out quite well as I approached.'

George, who had been left in charge, a grown boy on Christmas leave from his *Internat*, turned crimson. The cage-birds sank into resentful twittering.

'Fräulein, I offer you my condolences on all you have gone through, and must still go through,' said the old man, and then, turning to the little ones, 'Don't you give a thought to your step-sister? Can't you see that she looks very different now from formerly?'

'We thought so at first,' said Mimi, 'but now we can't remember what she looked like before.'

They are fortunate, thought Kegel.

'Let them stay, they must stay,' Sophie cried. 'Ach, you don't know how dull we were, except just at first, in Jena. And now that I am back home –'

'You do not expect Hardenberg?'

'We can't tell about his coming and going,' said George. 'He is one of the family, he does not need to give us notice.'

The Magister signed to the nursemaid to take Mimi and Rudolf away. He himself put one of the shawls over the birds, still flustered and faintly muttering in their cages. Then he sat down in the chair at the foot of the day-bed, and took out a book.

'Ach, Magister, my old *Fibel!*' shrieked Sophie.

'No, this is for more advanced pupils,' he said. 'These are passages which tell us what the ancient Romans, or some of them, wrote on the subject of friendship.'

'It is so good of you to come . . .' Sophie managed to say. 'I want you to pardon me . . . I couldn't bear to hurt you . . . I am not laughing now, or not nearly so much.'

'My feelings do not matter in the slightest degree. If they did, I should not have become a teacher.'

The Mandelsloh was at the door. 'Did you not know that on no account must Sophie laugh or cry until the wound is healed completely?'

'I swear I did not know that,' cried George in great distress.

'I am sure you did not,' said the Magister.

'I am so foolish,' said Sophie suddenly. 'I am not of much use in this world.'

Rockenthien had blundered in after the Mandelsloh. 'I have come to hear the lesson,' he called over her shoulder, adapting his voice, as he thought, to the sick room. 'I hope to benefit from it.'

'All who listen will benefit,' said Kegel. 'But half an hour will be sufficient for Fräulein Sophie.'

'That is what I have told them,' said Rockenthien.

'Of whom are you speaking?'

Of all of them, it seemed – everyone he had been able to gather together on the way up from his office – Mimi and Rudi once again, with their nursemaid, a young footman, two orphan girls who had been given work, for charity's sake, in the linen room and whose names nobody knew, the goats'-milk boy, who in ordinary circumstances never came into the house. Some hung back, but the Hausherr generously urged them on, telling them not to lose an opportunity which might come but once. 'I myself am not quite sure what Cicero said about friendship.' Sophie held out her arms to them all. In the racket her laughter and coughing could scarcely be heard. The little dogs, each desperate to be first, bounded back, with flattened ears, onto the bed to lick her face.

The Magister Kegel closed his book. 'After all, these people were born for joy,' he thought.

At the beginning of March 1797 Fritz had ten days official leave, which he spent at Grüningen. He asked Sophie: 'My dearest Philosophy, do you sleep well?'

'Oh, yes. They give me something.'

'The night is a dark power,' he said.

'Oh, I am not afraid of the night.'

On the evening of the 10th of March he said to the Mandelsloh, 'Should I stay here?'

'You must judge of that for yourself.'

'May I see her?'

'No, not now.'

'But later?'

The Mandelsloh, who appeared to have come to some sort of decision, said, 'At the moment, there is no healing. We were told yesterday to keep the wound open.'

'How?'

'With silk thread.'

'And for how long?'

'I don't know for how long.'

He asked once again:

'Should I stay here?' This time he got no answer and he cried out, 'Dear God, why does there have to be a bully like you, a lance-corporal masquerading as a woman, between me and my Söphgen?'

'You would not look at the wound,' said the Mandelsloh, 'but I don't hold that against you.'

'I don't want to hear about the things you don't hold against me. Am I to go or to stay?'

'We have talked about courage before,' the Mandelsloh reminded him.

'We agreed that it couldn't be measured absolutely,' Fritz said. 'The Bernhard was courageous when he ran away from us down to the river. The mother, in her way, was courageous when she met me in the garden —'

'What garden?'

'— Karl was under fire with his regiment at Mainz. And you, too, you were present at the three operations. And my Söphgen —'

'This is not a competition,' said the Mandelsloh. 'Anyway, it is of no use looking back. What can you do for her? That is all you have to ask yourself in this house.'

'If they would allow me to nurse her, although you may not believe me, I could do that,' said Fritz. 'Yes, about that I do know a little.'

'If you stayed here, you would not be wanted as a nurse,' the Mandelsloh replied. 'You would be wanted as a liar.'

Fritz raised his heavy head.

'What then should I say?'

'God help us, from day to day you would have to say to her – "You look a little better this morning, Söphgen. Yes, I think a little better. Soon you will be able to go out into the garden. Nothing is needed but some warmer weather."'

She spoke the words as players do at a first rehearsal, without emotion. Fritz looked at her with horror.

'And if I could not say that, would you think of me as a coward?'

'My idea of cowardice is very simple,' said the Mandelsloh.

After a moment Fritz cried out, 'I could not lie to her, any more than I could lie to myself.'

'I don't know to what extent a poet lies to himself.'

'She is my spirit's guide. She knows that.'

The Mandelsloh did not answer.

'Shall I stay?'

Still she said nothing, and Fritz went abruptly out of the room. Where will he go? the Mandelsloh wondered. That is so much simpler for a man. If a woman has something that is not easy to decide, where can she go to be alone?

Sophie was disappointed when she heard that Hardenberg had gone back to Weissenfels, but not excessively. Quite often before he had had to leave at a time when she was not well enough to see him. If she was awake, she could listen for the sound of his horse being brought round from the stable-yard to the front of the house, although he no longer rode the Gaul, whose dragging steps she had always been able to recognise. Sometimes he would be on the point of leaving and then dismount and run back again across the hall, up the two staircases which were nothing to him, into her room to say to her once again, 'Sophie, you are my heart's heart.'

This evening that was not the case, and he did not come back.

Three hours and three quarters to Weissenfels, with a stop at Freyburg. Outside Weissenfels the vegetable plots lay bare, except for the stalks of the winter cabbage, in the moonlight. The town gates were shut. Fritz paid the fine which was collected from latecomers, and rode slowly down to his father's house.

It was the first week in Lent, and only a few lights shone in the windows of the Kloster Gasse. At the house, his father and mother were already in bed. Erasmus was the only one of the family still up.

'I could not stay –' Fritz told him.

'Best of brothers –'

Afterword

SOPHIE died at half-past ten in the morning on the 19th of March, two days after her fifteenth birthday. Fritz, at Weissenfels, got the news two days later. Karoline Just also received a letter from one of Sophie's elder sisters, which described how the poor girl, 'in her fantasy', had kept thinking she heard the sound of horses' hooves.

Fritz did not become well-known as a writer until after Sophie's death. In the February of 1798, he told his friends that in future he would write under an old family name, Novalis, meaning 'clearer of new land'. As Novalis he published his *Hymns to the Night* and worked on a number of projects, some finished, some left in fragments. The story of the Blue Flower, now called *Heinrich von Ofterdingen*, was never finished.

In December 1798, Fritz became engaged to Julie, the daughter of Councillor Johann Friedrich von Charpentier, Professor of Mathematics at the Mining Academy of Freiberg. She was twenty-two years old. He was now doing well in the Salt Mine Directorate and had been appointed Supernumerary Magistrate in the District of Thuringia. To Friedrich Schlegel he wrote that a very interesting life appeared to await him. 'Still,' he added, 'I would rather be dead.'

At the end of the 1790s the young Hardenbergs, in their turn, began to go down, almost without protest, with pulmonary tuberculosis. Erasmus, who had insisted that he coughed blood only because he laughed too much, died on Good Friday, 1797. Sidonie lasted until the age of twenty-two. At the beginning of 1801 Fritz, who had been showing the same symptoms, went back to his parents' house in Weissenfels. As he lay dying he asked Karl to play the piano for him. When Friedrich Schlegel arrived Fritz told him that he had entirely changed his plan for the story of the Blue Flower.

The Bernhard was drowned in the Saale on the 28th of November 1800.

George was killed as First Lieutenant at the Battle of Smolensk in 1812.

A year after Fritz's death, Karoline Just was married to her cousin, Carl August.

The Mandelsloh was divorced from her husband in 1800 and married a General von Bose. She lived to be seventy-five.

Fritz's gold ring with its inscription 'Sophie be my Guardian Spirit' is in the Municipal Museum at Weissenfels.

PENELOPE FITZGERALD

Innocence

With an introduction by Julian Barnes

The Ridolfis are a Florentine family of long lineage and little money. It is 1955, and the family, like its decrepit villa and farm, has seen better days. Only eighteen-year-old Chiara shows anything like vitality.

Chiara has set her heart on Salvatore, a young and brilliant doctor who resolved long ago to be emotionally dependent on no one. Faced with this, she calls on her English girlfriend Barney to help her make the impossible match.

'Witty and moving . . . not just about Italians in love but of living and loving for all humans'   *The Times*

PENELOPE FITZGERALD

The Gate of Angels

Shortlisted for the Booker Prize

With an introduction by Philip Hensher

It is 1912, and at Cambridge University the modern age is knocking at the gate. Fred Fairly, a Junior Fellow at the college of St Angelicus – where for centuries no female has been allowed to set foot – lectures in physics. Science, he is certain, will explain everything. Until into Fred's orderly life comes Daisy. Fred is smitten. Why have I met her? He wonders. How can I tell if she's quite what she seems? Fred is a scientist. To him the truth should be everything. But even scientists make mistakes.

'Exquisite, moving, wonderful'   *Independent on Sunday*

PENELOPE FITZGERALD

The Beginning of Spring

Shortlisted for the Booker Prize

With an introduction by Andrew Miller

It is March 1913, and the grand old city of Moscow is stirring herself to meet the beginning of spring. Change is in the air and nowhere more so than at 22 Lipka Street, the home of English printer Frank Reid. Frank's wife Nellie has taken the train back to England, with no explanation, leaving him with their three young children. Into his life comes Lisa Ivanovna, a country girl, untroubled to the point of seeming simple. But is she? And why has Frank's accountant, Selwyn, gone to such lengths to bring them together?

'Flawless. Packed with the kind of off-beat humour and perceptive observation that makes you turn back and read it again'   *Sunday Times*

PENELOPE FITZGERALD

The Bookshop

Shortlisted for the Booker Prize

In the small East Anglian town of Hardborough, Florence Green decides, against polite but ruthless local opposition, to open a bookshop. Hardborough becomes a battleground. Florence has tried to change the way things have always been done and, as a result, she has to take on not only the people who have made themselves important, but natural and even supernatural forces too. Her fate will strike a chord with anyone who knows that life has treated them with less than justice.

'A gem, a vintage narrative ... a classic whose force has not merely lasted but has actually improved in the passage of years'
New York Times